SWITCHED

SWITCHED

Sienna Mercer

HarperTrophy®
An Imprint of HarperCollinsPublishers

With special thanks to Josh Greenhut

Harper Trophy® is a registered trademark
of HarperCollins Publishers.

My Sister the Vampire, Book One: Switched

Copyright © 2007 by Working Partners Limited
Series created by Working Partners Limited

www.harpercollinschildrens.com

Library of Congress Cataloging-in-Publication Data
Mercer, Sienna.
    Switched / by Sienna Mercer. — 1st HarperTrophy ed.
        p.   cm. — (My sister the vampire ; #1)
    Summary: Upon moving to Franklin Grove, eighth-
grader Olivia Abbott, a pink-loving cheerleader, learns that
she has a twin sister, Ivy Vega, whose "goth" appearance
hides a weird secret.
    ISBN 978-0-06-087113-0
    [1. Vampires—Fiction. 2. Sisters—Fiction. 3. Twins—
Fiction. 4. Schools—Fiction. 5. Cheerleading—Fiction.
6. Moving, Household—Fiction.] I. Title.
PZ7.M53328Swi 2007   2007011853
[Fic]—dc22   CIP
                                                                AC

Typography by Joel Tippie
❖
First Harper Trophy edition, 2007
12 13 CG/BR 20 19 18 17 16 15 14 13 12

For my brother, Jared, with love and gratitude

CHAPTER 1

Here we go, Olivia Abbott thought as her mother's car pulled away from the curb.

Olivia stood on the sidewalk and smoothed the skirt of her new pink dress for the millionth time. She usually felt her best in pink, but for some reason it wasn't helping at all this morning.

Olivia wished she didn't feel so nervous. After all, it wasn't like this was the cheerleading nationals or anything. It was just her first day of eighth grade at a new middle school. In an unfamiliar town. Where she didn't know anybody.

She was totally freaking out.

If it wasn't for her dad's new job, she'd be

skipping into her regular school with Mimi and Kara and the rest of the old squad, instead of being the friendless new girl who shows up out of nowhere five weeks into the school year.

But, *whatever*, Olivia was determined to make the best of the situation. This would be just like the first time she ate sushi. It would be weird for a second—unfamiliar and slightly funny smelling—but then she'd grow to love it. Besides, what was she going to do, cry until high school?

Olivia stood up straight and clapped her hands twice, like at the beginning of a cheer. Then, with her mouth set in a smile, she made her way bravely toward the front entrance.

Her old school had been a modern box, painted a combination of ugly beige and ugly brown, but Franklin Grove Middle School was different. It looked a thousand years old. Ivy dripped from the huge entryway columns, and beyond the enormous oak front doors was a hallway so big you could make a sixteen-person pyramid across it. Olivia's old school was plastered with inspirational posters with sayings that made no sense, like LIVE EVERY DAY LIKE IT'S TODAY!

Here, black-and-white school photographs hung on the walls dating back to practically the ice age. She passed one picture with a plaque that said CONVOCATION 1912. It showed a bunch of serious-looking students in black robes.

At least the sound of everyone rushing to their first class was familiar: lockers clanging, sneakers squeaking, people laughing. Olivia made her way through the bustle. There seemed to be a lot more Goths here than there had been at her old school. They were as black-and-white as the photographs on the walls: black clothes, pale skin, heavy black boots.

Olivia caught her own reflection in a display case. Her pretty dress floated, ghostlike, in front of tarnished trophies and a dark banner that said GO, FRANKLIN GROVE DEVILS! She tried to keep smiling, but her heart fell. She looked like a lollipop in a graveyard. What if she never managed to fit in here?

"Rise and shine," a voice interrupted. Startled, Olivia realized she was standing right in the way of a Goth girl. A prickly bun atop the girl's head was held in place by a wooden spike—*Cool,* Olivia thought, *a chopstick!*—and she wore a black dress with a neat slanted hem that started just above one knee and ended at the opposite ankle.

Olivia stepped to the left, trying to get out of the way, but the girl had the same idea. They both stepped in the other direction. Then they both stepped back again. Olivia laughed apologetically, but the girl just looked at her in a weird way. It wasn't mean or anything. She just looked curious, sort of like an inquisitive black cat.

"Do I . . ." the girl began, frowning. "Are you new here?"

"How can you tell?" Olivia asked jokingly.

"So you're probably looking for the office, right?" the girl replied, with the faintest of smiles, as another Goth in a black T-shirt that said HOP, BUNNY, HOP! in pink letters pulled up, a digital camera hanging around her neck. The first girl nodded to her friend before pointing Olivia in the right direction. "To the end, around the corner, office is on the right."

Olivia had been going the wrong way completely. "Thanks," she said sheepishly. "I probably would have been wandering the halls looking for the principal's office until I got sent to the principal's office for wandering the halls!"

To her relief, both Goths cracked a smile. Then the one with the stick in her hair looked at Olivia like she was trying to remember something. Finally she shrugged. "Well, good luck." And with that, she and her friend walked off down the hallway.

The office was exactly where the girl said it would be.

"Have a seat over there," the gray-haired receptionist said. "Principal Whitehead will be with you in just a minute."

Olivia turned around and saw a chair, next to where a girl with long, soft-looking, curly blond hair was sitting, reading a thick, battered paperback. The girl wore jeans and a yellow T-shirt, and on the floor at her feet was a canvas bag with a button on the strap that said ALIEN SPAWN ARE PEOPLE, TOO.

Finally, Olivia thought, *someone who isn't wearing black!* She walked over and held out her hand. "Hi. Olivia Abbott."

The girl lifted her eyes from her book. She

looked confused. "No, actually, my name's Camilla. Camilla Edmunson."

Olivia laughed. "No. I mean *my* name's Olivia," she explained. "Nice to meet you, Camilla."

Camilla made an I'm-such-a-dork face and shook Olivia's hand. "Sorry. I'm just *really* into this book."

Olivia sat down. "Isn't that the best? When you get so caught up in a book that you're, like, in a different world?"

"I know!" said Camilla eagerly. She held up the cover of her paperback: *Random Access* by Coal Knightley, The Second Book in The Cyborg Trilogy. "Ever read it?"

"Nope. Is it any good?" Olivia asked.

"Are you kidding?" Camilla cried. "This is my third time through!"

"That's exactly how I am with the Count Vira books." Olivia sighed. "You know—vampires, bloodsucking, frilly collars. They're sort of my secret vice."

"Don't worry." Camilla grinned. "Your secret's safe with me. As long as you don't tell anyone I can speak the Cyborg Beta language."

Olivia laughed. "It's a deal!"

The principal appeared, looking like school principals everywhere: bald head, short sleeves, bad tie.

"Olivia Abbott?" he said. "Welcome to Franklin Grove."

★ 🦇 ★

Ivy Vega could have bitten her best friend, Sophia Hewitt, for abandoning her as they got to social studies. So what if they were almost late? That didn't mean Sophia had to rush to her desk the moment they arrived, leaving Ivy zombified in the doorway as the second bell rang.

Ivy clutched at the dark emerald ring hanging on the charm around her neck, hoping it would ward off her fear like a magic amulet. As if. It had been three weeks since Ms. Starling assigned seats, and Ivy still felt like she was caught in direct sunlight without any sunblock. Sitting at a desk next to drop-dead Brendan Daniels each morning was *torture*. Quite enjoyable torture, admittedly, but still.

She forced herself to put one foot in front of the other, shooting Sophia her meanest look—the death squint—as she crept past. Sophia rolled her eyes.

Ivy pulled the long wooden spike out of her bun as she sat down, then peered out at Brendan from behind a curtain of dark hair.

He was utterly Goth gorgeous in every way: skin the color of pure white marble, high cheekbones that made dark valleys in his face, curly black hair that hung near his shoulders. Her heart convulsed. She was sure she'd turn to dust if they ever exchanged a single word. He clicked his mechanical pencil.

I'm going to fail this class, thought Ivy. *How can I concentrate on a single thing when he's so close?*

A singsong voice interrupted her thoughts. "After I win the cheerleading tryouts and become squad captain of the Devils, I'm totally going to do the best cheers ever!" said Charlotte Brown.

Kill me now, Ivy thought. Ivy could think of only one thing more painful than unrequited love, and it was hearing Charlotte Brown babble on about herself.

"I am already so much better than my big

sister," Charlotte twittered, "and she's, like, co-captain of the varsity squad at Franklin High."

"Maybe I'll be *your* co-captain!" one of Charlotte's minions said brightly.

"Maybe I won't *have* a co-captain," replied Charlotte coolly.

It was one thing to get assigned a seat next to Brendan Daniels and die of embarrassment. But it was another thing altogether to get seated behind Charlotte Brown and die of boredom listening to her endless, dumb, mean-spirited chatter. Charlotte and her lemmings had been yammering on about cheerleading tryouts nonstop since the first day of school.

Ivy pushed her hair behind her ears and pulled out her notebook. She angled herself away from Brendan—if she couldn't spend eternity with him, she could at least use the time productively—and turned to the back page, where she jotted her ideas for the school paper.

"Former Franklin Grove Cheerleading Captains: Where Are They Now?" she wrote. *Let's see,* she thought. There was Carli Spith, who was now

9

a cashier at FoodMart. And Melinda Willsocks, who got crowned Miss Revoline at the auto show last year but still lived with her parents and couldn't get a regular job. And . . .

Ivy realized that the room had suddenly gone quiet. She stopped writing.

"Class," Ms. Starling announced, "I'd like to introduce you to a new member of the Franklin Grove community."

Beside Ms. Starling stood the girl in the pink dress. Ivy got the same weird feeling she'd had when she'd first seen her in the hall—like déjà vu mixed with indigestion.

"Her name is Olivia Abbott," Ms. Starling explained. "She's just moved here from the coast."

Ivy put her hand on her necklace and twirled her ring as she watched the new girl at the front of the room. Olivia's long brown hair was pulled back in a ponytail. Her dress was seriously pink. She wasn't the kind of person who would normally attract Ivy's attention. So why did Ivy feel like she was looking at someone she had met before?

Olivia was given a desk right near the front, probably because, once again, Ms. Starling was determined to ruin Ivy's life using the ancient curse of assigned seating; no matter how she craned her neck, Ivy was unable to catch another glimpse of the new girl's face.

In between trying to learn about the legislative branch of government and trying to look cool and beautiful in case Brendan was looking at her, Ivy tried to figure out how she knew Olivia Abbott.

She decided to list all the possibilities in her notebook: Kindergarten? Elementary school? Dance camp? Summer retreat? Meat & Greet Diner? Costume ball? Mall? Finally, desperately, Ivy wrote . . . *TV* ???

There weren't many people Ivy knew who Sophia wouldn't recognize as well, so Ivy tore a blank corner from one page and passed a note back to her friend while Ms. Starling was writing on the blackboard.

Sophia's response came at once: "R u kidding? She's 2 pink 4 us 2 know!" She'd drawn one of her bunny cartoons at the bottom.

"*Love* your fur!" one bunny said.

"Pink is totally my natural color!" replied another, which had a ribbon in its hair.

Ivy tried to cloak her laughter with a fake cough, but the resulting rattle was seriously grave. Brendan probably thought she sounded like a cat coughing up a fur ball.

Ivy saw Olivia raise her hand to ask a question. "Do we have to type the assignment?" Even her voice sounded familiar.

Ivy was more certain than ever that there was *something* strange about the girl in the pink dress.

When the bell rang, Ivy waited for Brendan to leave before she got up. She and Sophia were headed to their lockers when Sophia nudged her arm and said, "Looks like the new bunny's about to be roadkill."

Down the hall, Olivia Abbott was standing by the bathrooms, surrounded by four boys in black heavy metal T-shirts.

Oh no, thought Ivy. It was the Beasts.

Before she knew what she was doing, Ivy was rushing toward the group.

"New meat," she heard one of the boys say.

"Yeah, dude." Another Beast chuckled. "Like,

with ketchup. I wonder if she likes horror stories."
They all guffawed.

For the first time, Ivy saw Olivia without a smile on her face. Their eyes met over the boys' shoulders. Olivia looked half confused, half scared.

Ivy clenched her teeth. As night was her witness, there was *no way* she was going to let this girl be eaten alive by the biggest Goth losers at Franklin. "Buzz off and die, Beasts!" she growled, shoving them aside and stepping in front of Olivia. "Go haunt a convenience store parking lot."

"What's your problem, Vega?"

"You're my problem, you rat. Now put a stake in it." Ivy unleashed her death squint. "I *said* buzz off!"

The Beasts laughed uncomfortably before slinking away down the hall.

"I am *so* happy you showed up," Olivia blurted. "I don't even know your name, and you're already my favorite person!"

Ivy introduced herself. "And don't worry about the Beasts," she said. "They're harmless.

They act all grave, but they're not nearly as scary as they smell."

"You sure seem to know how to handle them," Olivia remarked.

"Yeah, well, I'd better," Ivy said. "I'm going to have to put up with them *forever*."

Olivia laughed. "Anyway, thank you for the second time today, Ivy Vega. I'm really grateful."

That strange feeling rushed back over Ivy with a force so powerful she nearly stumbled. All at once, she realized why the new girl looked so familiar. *She looks a lot like me,* Ivy thought. *More than a lot—she looks almost* exactly *like me!*

A wave of nausea hit her, and her knees trembled. She was either going to throw up or faint right in the middle of the hall. Brendan would see her splayed out on the linoleum floor, her face whiter than bone, her black-stockinged legs twisted like a doll's.

Olivia was still talking, but the roar in Ivy's head was too loud for her to hear.

"Later," Ivy croaked. And, quick as a bat, she flew into the girls' bathroom.

 CHAPTER 2

Oh great, Olivia thought, *I overdid it.* Why did she always have to come on so strong when she met new people? Here was this girl, Ivy, clearly trying to be nice, and Olivia immediately started talking her ear off. The poor girl had looked like she was about to puke.

Still, Olivia couldn't help wondering why Ivy Vega had gone out of her way to help her. After all, Ivy was ultra Goth. For someone like her to be friendly to someone like Olivia twice in one morning was unusual to say the least.

Whatever. Olivia had gym next, and she needed to find the locker room and change as fast as she could. The principal had said that Ms. Barnett, her PE teacher, was also the cheerleading coach, and Olivia wanted to make a stellar first impression.

"You're not wearing socks, Miss Abbott," Ms. Barnett said sternly less than seven minutes later. Olivia had barely had a chance to introduce herself. "This is a physical education class, young lady. How can you receive a physical education if your feet are not properly attired?"

Olivia made sure she kept smiling, which wasn't easy considering she was also trying to nod seriously. "I completely agree," she said sincerely. "I've been cheerleading since I was eight, and I fully understand the dangers of painful blisters and unwanted foot fungus. I promise not to forget my socks again, ma'am."

Ms. Barnett nodded with begrudging respect.

There isn't a female gym teacher on earth who doesn't love being called Ma'am, thought Olivia.

After Ms. Barnett had given her the details of the squad tryouts coming up in three weeks, she led Olivia across the gym to where three girls were taking turns doing handsprings. She gestured to one with a blond ponytail, who bounced right over.

"Charlotte Brown, this is Olivia Abbott. She's also interested in trying out for the squad."

"You're the new girl!" Charlotte cried. "Welcome to Fraaaaaaaanklin"—she rolled her hands like a motor and threw her arms in the air—"GROVE!"

Olivia smiled. "Nice to meet you."

"Come on," said Charlotte. "I'm just about to teach Katie and Allison this unbelievably awesome cheer!"

For the first time all morning, Olivia let herself relax. She'd found the cheerleaders. Unlike the other students in gym class, all three girls wore matching short pink shorts and tight gray Franklin Devils T-shirts. Olivia just knew she'd be having sleepovers and talking about boys in the locker room with them before long.

Olivia watched Charlotte run through the routine. The girl clearly knew her stuff. She had good energy, sharp moves, nice tumbling. It was completely possible that Charlotte Brown was going to be her new best friend.

"That was great, Charlotte!" Olivia said. *Except,* she thought, *"devil" doesn't really rhyme with "bubble," but, whatever.* "We used to do a cheer a lot like that at my old school."

"I wrote it myself." Charlotte beamed.

The routine had some complicated parts but nothing too difficult. Olivia got it in no time. After a few run-throughs, she even tried some new lines, shouting, "You know you're a Devil when you raise the noise level!" instead of Charlotte's words.

"Sorry, Olivia," Charlotte said, running over from where she was working with Katie and Allison on the handclaps. "I think you got the words wrong. We'd better do it again." Which was fine. After all, it was Charlotte's cheer.

Olivia was just relieved to feel that she fit in. In fact, at the end of class, she was on her way to the locker room when Ms. Barnett actually smiled at her.

"Nice cheering, Olivia," said the gym teacher. Olivia could have done a flip on the spot!

"Ms. Barnett says that to everyone," Charlotte

said, as she pushed open the door to the locker room.

Olivia shrugged. "Hey, this morning I was no one. 'Everyone' is a step up!"

* 🦇 *

It sure didn't feel that way at lunch, though. Looking out at the cafeteria, Olivia felt like no one again. She had no idea where to sit. She wished she were back at her old school, with Kara and Mimi waving at her from their table by the window.

Finally, Olivia spotted Camilla sitting by herself in the corner, devouring her sci-fi epic along with her lunch. Olivia almost took off running, she was so happy to see her.

She was almost at Camilla's table when Charlotte Brown appeared, wearing a pink sweater. Behind her stood Katie and Allison, their smiles shining like white billboards above their trays.

"Come sit with us!" Charlotte said.

Olivia glanced over at Camilla, whose nose was still buried in her book. For some reason, Olivia's stomach sank. "Okay."

"This is the popular table," Katie told her as they sat down.

"We sit here every day," said Allison.

"Great." Olivia smiled, silently noting that they were the only people at the table.

"Girls," Charlotte said. "First things first. I think it's our duty to tell Olivia the rules."

"Which rules?" Olivia asked.

"Duh." Katie rolled her eyes. "Charlotte's rules."

"*No*, Katie." Charlotte looked annoyed. "The rules of Franklin Grove Middle School." She straightened her back and took a deep breath. "Rule number one," Charlotte announced. She reached over to Olivia's tray and gingerly picked up a piece of garlic bread with two fingers. She looked completely grossed out, as if she were holding a dead bird. "*Never* order garlic bread. It totally kills . . ."

Vampires? Olivia wondered.

". . . your social life," Charlotte finished, dropping the bread so that it landed back on Olivia's tray with a thud.

"Rule number two," Charlotte went on, wiping

her hands on her napkin. "Pink is in. Black"—she shot a cold look at another table, where Olivia saw Ivy Vega sitting with some friends—"is *so* last season. But you already knew that, right?" Charlotte added and winked.

"I so can't wait to borrow that dress," Katie said, looking Olivia up and down approvingly.

"Anyway," said Charlotte, "rule number two is: Pink is perfect!"

Olivia shifted in her seat uncomfortably.

"But rule number three," Charlotte continued, "is the most important rule of all."

Charlotte looked at Katie and Allison, who nodded solemnly. Then Charlotte did a double clap, and all three spoke in unison: "The squad is everything, and the captain makes the calls!"

It was as if they'd practiced it—which, Olivia realized, they probably had. "Cool," she said, not wanting to be mean. "Who's the captain?"

Katie and Allison looked at Olivia like she'd just popped a zit right at the table.

"It's all right," Charlotte said. "She's new. That's a perfectly good question, Olivia. *I'm* the captain."

Olivia couldn't help it; she was shocked. She had to eat a forkful of fruit salad just to cover her reaction. Finally she swallowed. "I, um, talked to Ms. Barnett in gym, and she said that the captainship won't be decided until tryouts."

"I know," said Charlotte, nodding sympathetically. "She actually *has* to say that or else she'll be fired. Like, to be fair. But everyone knows it's going to be me."

"It's just like everyone on the squad has to try out again every year, so it at least *looks* like new people have a chance," Katie said.

"Like you!" Allison chimed. Then she realized what she'd just said and added quickly, "Although I'm sure you'll make it if you stick with us."

Olivia forced herself to smile and nod. *I should have sat with Camilla,* she thought. And then, out of the corner of her eye, Olivia saw Ivy and her friends about to pass by, carrying their trays.

Charlotte cleared her throat. "It's such a shame," she said ultraloud, "when people can't afford to buy clothes from this century. We should totally set up a charity."

Oh, my gosh. Charlotte did not *just say that!* Olivia thought. She stared down at her tray as Ivy brushed past with her friends. Luckily, they didn't say anything.

When the Goths had gone, Olivia sat up straight. "Charlotte, what was all that about?"

"Excuse me?" Charlotte said haughtily.

"That girl, Ivy, saved my butt this morning. And even if she didn't, I don't really think that entitles you to smash her feelings."

"Well, thank you for *feedback*, Olivia," Charlotte huffed. "But it's clear you don't know what you're talking about. Now, I'll forgive you for not knowing this because you're new, but let me tell you something about those Goths. The walking dead don't *have* feelings!"

★ 🦇 ★

How utterly great, Ivy thought grimly as the bell rang for the last class of the day. *The new girl— who looks just like me but is best friends with Charlotte Brown—is in my science class, too.*

Ivy slumped in her chair in the back row. She could not believe Olivia had been sucked into

Charlotte's web so easily. Olivia might share Ivy's nose, but that was obviously where the resemblance ended.

Uh-oh. Olivia was coming over.

"Hi," Olivia said quietly. She seemed embarrassed.

She should be! thought Ivy.

Olivia said, "Mr. Strain told me you're my lab partner."

What?! This is so unbelievably O-negative, Ivy raged silently. She was now officially having the weirdest and worst day ever. She was ready to say something really grave, but the look on Olivia's face stopped her.

"I am so horrified by what Charlotte said at lunch. I mean, you are, like, the nicest person I've met so far. I know I should have said something on the spot. It's just that, I don't know, I was so *shocked*. I mean, look at you. You've got unbelievable style," Olivia said.

"P-pardon me?" Ivy stammered.

"That's the coolest dress I've seen all day!" Olivia went on. "And I'm absolutely going to try the chopstick-in-the-hair thing. You've got *way* more style than Charlotte Brown."

Ivy was speechless.

"Anyway," Olivia concluded, "I'm really sorry."

Maybe Olivia Abbott wasn't a cheerleader underling after all. Ivy moved her books aside so Olivia could sit down.

"It's okay," Ivy said. "I'm used to Charlotte's petty ways. I bet she didn't tell you I'm her next-door neighbor."

"Are you serious?" Olivia asked incredulously.

"Dead serious. And she never misses an opportunity to say something nasty." Ivy rolled her eyes. "I guess it's a cheerleader thing."

Olivia shook her head firmly. "I cheered at my old school, and most cheerleaders aren't like that—any more than Goth girls are all witches."

"As if." Ivy laughed, impressed.

Olivia opened her notebook. "I mean, it would be one thing if you'd *done* something. But for Charlotte to act like that out of nowhere—"

"Actually," Ivy interrupted, "there *was* sixth grade."

Olivia's eyes widened. "What happened in sixth grade?"

"I tried—"

Mr. Strain appeared in front of their desk. "Don't you two think you should be preparing your lab materials like the rest of the class?"

"Sorry," they both mumbled. Ivy sheepishly handed a pair of safety goggles to Olivia. A few moments later, when Mr. Strain had gone, she continued in a whisper, "I tried out for cheerleading."

"*YOU* tried out—" Olivia gasped, but Ivy motioned for Olivia to keep her voice down. "For *cheerleading*?" Olivia finished in a whisper.

"Yep." Ivy smiled. "My dad wanted me to have an extracurricular. I actually made the squad. But, guess . . . who . . . didn't?"

"No way." Olivia's jaw dropped.

"Way." Ivy grinned. "Charlotte was only first alternate."

"You can cheer?" Olivia asked.

"I may not be a smiler, but I *am* really good at gymnastics," Ivy replied.

"You can too smile," objected Olivia.

"Yes, but I don't *like* to smile," Ivy said. "And I certainly don't like to be perky. Truth is, I wasn't really into the 'cheer' part of cheerleading."

Olivia wrinkled her nose. "That part *is* really important," she admitted.

"It just wasn't my style," Ivy explained. "Even my dad knew it. So, after the first week, I quit and joined the newspaper."

"And what happened?" probed Olivia.

"Charlotte got to fill the spot I left. That was the only reason she made the squad. She's never gotten over it. And the rest, as they say—"

"Is middle school!" Olivia blurted. They both laughed.

"Ladies!" Mr. Strain interrupted from across the room. "Please focus on the experiment at hand! We are exploring the combustion of plant matter, not your social lives!"

Olivia made a face and raised her hand to turn on the Bunsen burner. There was a dark emerald ring on her middle finger.

The strange feeling Ivy had experienced earlier when she'd looked at Olivia rushed back over her like a tidal wave. Her hand instantly flew to her neck, and she felt for the ring on its chain beneath her dress. She found it near her throat. But how could there be two of them? The ring was the only thing she had from her real parents. She was sure it was one of a kind. How could Olivia have one, too?

"Ivy?" Olivia was staring at her. "Are you okay?"

Somehow Ivy forced herself to smile. "F-fine," she stammered.

Ivy didn't know how she would make it to the end of class, but she did. When the bell finally rang, she grabbed Olivia's arm. "Come with me!"

"Sure," Olivia said. "Where to?"

Ivy looked around wildly as they stepped into the hallway. "The bathroom."

Ivy thought she would die if there was anybody else in the girls' bathroom. She checked to make sure it was completely empty.

"Are you going to tell me a secret?" Olivia asked as she watched curiously. Ivy came over and turned Olivia to face the mirror.

Olivia's eyes met Ivy's in the reflection, and all at once, Olivia's smile disappeared. "Ivy, what is it?"

Ivy lifted Olivia's wrist so they could both see her hand in the mirror. "Where did you get this ring?" Ivy asked, her voice trembling.

Olivia looked stunned for a moment. Then she took a deep breath. "It's the only thing in the world," she said slowly, "that my real parents gave me."

Ivy reached carefully into her dress, pulled out her chain, and held up her ring next to Olivia's.

The rings were identical. They had the same ornate etchings on the same heavy platinum bands, the same oddly cut green emeralds. They even seemed to shine brighter now that they were next to each other.

Ivy and Olivia's eyes reconnected in the mirror.

When Ivy spoke again, her voice was almost a whisper. "When's your birthday?"

Olivia's voice shook. "May . . ." she began.

"Thirteenth," Ivy finished.

Olivia put her hand to her mouth. "You look just like me!"

"*You* look just like *me*," Ivy said, raising her eyebrows.

Olivia spun around to face her.

"Who were . . ." they both started.

"How did . . ." Neither of them finished.

Ivy took a deep breath.

"When were . . ." they said as one.

"Okay," Ivy cried. "You go first."

"Are you adopted?" Olivia blurted. "I am."

"Me, too," Ivy answered. "How old were you?"

"One," Olivia replied. "You?"

"Same."

"Where were you born?" Olivia asked.

"Owl Creek, Tennessee," Ivy told her.

"Me, too!" Olivia shook her head. "This is so out of control."

"Have you ever been there?" asked Ivy.

Olivia's eyes lit up. "Once, a few years ago. My parents drove through on the way to Nashville. There's not much there except these unbelievably huge trees."

"You have no idea how jealous I am." Ivy sighed. She'd always wanted to go to Owl Creek.

"What about your ring?" Olivia asked.

"I got it for my tenth birthday," Ivy replied. "My father said my real parents wanted it that way. It was a condition of the adoption."

"That's exactly what my parents told me!" Olivia bit her lip. "Do you . . . do you know anything else about them?" She looked at Ivy hopefully.

Ivy's heart sank. "No. My dad never even met them," she said. "How about you?"

"No." Olivia sighed.

For a moment, they were both quiet. Then Ivy's mouth curled into a wide grin. "Well, Olivia, I've always wanted an evil twin."

Olivia rolled her eyes. "That is just what *I* was going to say!"

CHAPTER 3

For as long as she could remember, Olivia had wished for a sister. Now she didn't know which was hardest to believe: the fact that she had a sister, the fact that she had a *twin* sister, or the fact that her twin sister was her lab partner in science.

Studying Ivy's face, she felt dumb for not realizing right away. Underneath the dark eyeliner and Goth outfit, Ivy looked exactly like her: the angular nose, the oval chin, the arching eyebrows. And to think Olivia had been scared she wouldn't find anyone like herself at Franklin Grove!

"We need to talk," Ivy said. She even had the same smile as Olivia. "Want to walk to the Meat & Greet for a bite?"

"Sure. I'm starved!" Olivia beamed. "I just have to call my mom so she doesn't worry."

"Use my cell," Ivy said, reaching into her bag.

Olivia called home and said she'd be late because she was going out to eat with this really cool girl she'd met at school.

"That's great!" her mom replied. "I knew you'd have no trouble making new friends, Olivia. Make sure you're home by seven, and have fun!"

"What about calling your parents?" Olivia asked Ivy.

"It's always been just Dad and me," Ivy explained. "And he lets me be pretty independent."

Olivia and Ivy got their bags from their lockers, then headed down the hallway and out through the front doors of the school. The beginning of football season was Olivia's favorite time of year, and not just because of cheerleading. It felt like summer and smelled like fall. As they made their way down the street, Olivia looked over at Ivy walking beside her. The sun made shimmering patterns on her sister's black dress.

"Don't you think it's weird," Olivia mused, "that my dad just happened to be transferred to Franklin Grove?"

"I was thinking about that, too," Ivy said, doing a hopscotch hop over a crack in the sidewalk, "and I think there's only one explanation." She stopped and turned to Olivia. "I think we were meant to find each other."

Olivia's heart did a roundoff, and her eyes filled with tears. She gave Ivy a huge hug. She couldn't help it.

Ivy didn't move. *Oh, no*, Olivia thought. She was coming on too strong again. Or Ivy didn't want a sister. Or Ivy didn't want *her* as a sister.

But then Ivy hugged her back.

They both started sobbing right there in the middle of the sidewalk. If somebody had walked by, that person would have wondered what was wrong. But nothing was wrong. Everything was right. They were just thirteen-year-old twin sisters hugging for the first time.

Finally, Olivia let go and reached into her bag for some tissues. She blew her nose loudly. "Sorry if I snotted on your shoulder," she said.

Ivy smiled tearily. "Don't be sorry," she said, wiping black mascara tearstains from her cheeks. "I think I might have ruined your dress."

Olivia peered down at the smear of black on her bright pink sleeve. She couldn't help laughing. "You Goths really don't like pink, do you?"

Ivy chuckled as they walked on again. "I hope you like Franklin Grove," she said to Olivia. "The bunny population here isn't too bad."

Olivia laughed. "Yeah, I saw that T-shirt your friend was wearing. So what's it all about? Is this place infested with wild bunnies? I once read that when rabbits were introduced into Australia they, like, ruined the whole country."

"Very funny," Ivy said.

"No, really. I mean, their whole ecosystem was destroyed. The rabbits ate all the crops."

Ivy shook her head. "No, not *those* bunnies, the—" Suddenly Ivy went quiet.

Olivia glanced at her. She had a weird look in her eyes. "What's up?" Olivia asked.

"Huh?" her sister said distractedly. "Nothing. I was just . . . I was . . . thinking again about how strange it is . . ." She was talking really slowly. Then, all at once, she seemed to come back to life. "That we're *sisters*."

"No kidding!" Olivia agreed. "Why do you think we weren't adopted as a pair? I mean, don't they usually try to keep twins together?"

Ivy played with the ring around her neck. "I don't know," she said thoughtfully. "Do you have any other brothers or sisters?"

"No. Do you?" Olivia asked.

"No. Maybe both our parents could only adopt one kid. Or maybe our real parents wanted us apart." Ivy shrugged. "We don't know a thing about them."

Olivia nodded and followed Ivy toward the neon sign of the Meat & Greet Diner up ahead. "All *I* know is," Olivia said, "when I think that we could have been together for the last thirteen years, it makes me want to scream. I totally could've used a twin sister in second grade."

"Yeah," said Ivy as they crossed the parking lot. "Second grade *did* bite."

The restaurant was packed with other students from Franklin Grove Middle School. The place was decorated like a meat locker, with hooks hanging from the ceiling. But instead of slabs of meat, they held cool things like piñatas and disco balls. Olivia followed Ivy to an empty booth hidden in an alcove near the back of the restaurant.

A waitress decked out in a butcher's apron appeared. "The usual?" she asked Ivy.

"Definitely," Ivy replied. "What about you, Olivia?"

The waitress looked over expectantly.

"What are you having?" Olivia asked Ivy.

Ivy put her finger on Olivia's open menu. "The Sink Your Teeth into This. It's an almost raw burger. It's utterly dripping," she said happily.

Gross, thought Olivia. She wrinkled her nose and turned back to the waitress. "I'll have the Bunny's Delight please." *What is it about bunnies in this town?* she wondered.

"You want salsa on your tofu burger?" the waitress asked.

"Yes, please," Olivia replied. "Oh, and salad dressing on the side."

She hoped the sight of Ivy's raw burger didn't make her nauseous. They might be twins, but they certainly didn't have the same tastes.

"Considering we're identical twins," Ivy said, "we've turned out seriously different."

"Oh, my gosh, I was just thinking that!" Olivia said. She cocked her head. "It must be a real trip for you to see what you'd look like in pastels, huh?"

They both laughed so loudly that the people in a nearby booth looked around to see what was so funny.

This time, Olivia thought blissfully, *I definitely sat at the right table!*

* 🦇 *

Ivy's stomach was still fluttering, and it wasn't because she'd laughed too hard or wolfed down her burger. It was because she had a twin sister.

When she really thought about it, she realized that she'd always known. That was the feeling that had come over her the first time she saw Olivia in the hallway this morning. It wasn't just the strange sensation of seeing someone who looks like you; it was the rush of seeing someone you'd waited your whole life to see again.

Except for one grave thing: How come Olivia didn't know what a bunny was? They were identical twins, right? So shouldn't they be *identical*?

If she doesn't know, thought Ivy, *I can't tell her.*

"Hello, Olivia," said a familiar high-pitched voice.

Ivy looked up. *Oh, yippee*, she thought sarcastically. *Charlotte Brown.*

"Hi, Charlotte," Olivia said.

"I'm sitting over there with Katie and Allison," Charlotte announced.

Olivia smiled blandly. "Say hi for me."

Charlotte turned her back to Ivy and bent down, like she was going to tell Olivia a secret. "I think you should know, Olivia," she said loud enough for Ivy to hear, "the Devils cheerleaders are like a really close group of highly elite girls. And hanging out with *certain people*"—she made quotation marks with her pink nails—"won't really help you become part of the club at all."

Ivy rolled her eyes and took a sip of her lemonade. *What a jerk!* she thought.

"Actually, Charlotte," Olivia replied in her own confiding tone, "I'm not sure if *you* know, but Ivy here is a huge fan of cheerleading. In fact, we were just talking about how good she looks in pastels!"

Ivy snorted, and her drink almost came out of her nose.

"Puh-lease," hooted Charlotte. "I don't think Ivy Vega could ever wear anything but black rags." She turned around to look down at Ivy. "Sorry," she said airily, "but you'll never be anything but a drab Goth loser."

"You shouldn't judge people by appearances," Ivy said icily.

"Oh, really? Then how come Jeff Moore, the coolest, hottest, cutest guy at school, has asked me to sit with him at lunch tomorrow?" Charlotte demanded.

"Because he wants to throw up?" Ivy suggested.

Charlotte grimaced and turned back to face Olivia, who hid her smile just in time. "The reason I came over here, Olivia," she said pointedly, "was to invite you to join us at lunch tomorrow. Katie and Allison are going to be there. I suggest you be there, too." She shot a grave look at Ivy.

"*Alone*." And, with that, Charlotte stomped back across the diner.

Ivy was so mad she felt like screaming. "If I wanted, I could be just as big a fashion victim as Charlotte Brown!" she fumed.

Olivia waved to the waitress and ordered a huge piece of chocolate cake with two forks. She leaned forward conspiratorially. "Sure. You'd make a great fashion victim, Ivy," she agreed. A smile crept across her face. "I should know."

"How come you look like a cat who just swallowed a bat?" Ivy asked suspiciously.

"Because I have an idea . . ." Her sister looked around to make sure no one was listening. "Since no one else knows about us, I think you should pretend to be me at lunch tomorrow," Olivia said with grin.

"What?" Ivy demanded.

"Think about it, Ivy. How funny would it be if Charlotte went through a whole meal surrounded by all her best friends—including her new BF, me? Except that *me* will be *you*!"

It's a killer idea, Ivy thought excitedly, *but it'll*

never work. "There's no way we could pull it off," she said, shaking her head. "I mean, we're twins, but we're not—"

"Identical?" Olivia interrupted.

"Okay. We're identical," Ivy conceded. "But we have very, very different . . . looks."

"Nothing that a little spray-on tan won't fix," Olivia countered.

"You're serious," Ivy said incredulously.

"Dead serious," Olivia replied.

That's exactly what I would have said, Ivy thought.

"My Kinski denim skirt would look *so hot* on you!" Olivia said eagerly.

Ivy tried not to smile, since she was still playing devil's advocate. "Okay, but what about the perky factor?" she asked. "It's not like I can smile and eat cafeteria Jell-O at the same time like you can. My cover would be blown in seconds."

"Don't worry." Olivia reached over and put her hand on top of Ivy's. "I'll coach you. Besides, what better way is there for twin sisters to get to know each other than to *be* each other?"

Olivia's emerald ring sparkled at Ivy.

That decides it, Ivy thought. She leaned forward

and said, "This is going to suck!"

Olivia's face fell. "You mean you won't do it?"

"No." Ivy shook her head. "'Suck' is good! 'Suck' is *really* good!"

"Oh," Olivia said. "Weird. So you'll do it?"

"I'll do it." Ivy grinned.

"In that case, I'd like to propose a toast." Olivia held up her glass. "To Ivy Vega, my twin sister."

Ivy raised her lemonade. "To Olivia Abbott, *my* twin sister."

They clinked their glasses. And then, at exactly the same moment, Ivy and her sister both laughed. "You suck!" they chorused.

CHAPTER 4

The next day, Olivia made her way to the science hall bathroom—which Ivy had chosen because it was the least-frequented bathroom in the school—and excitedly arranged her supplies on the counter: Santa Monica spray-on tan, Autumn Day blush, Shimmer lip gloss, Nature's Sheen hair gel . . . .

The door opened a crack, and Ivy's pale face appeared. She slipped inside and pulled a piece of cardboard out of her black patent leather purse.

Olivia's eyes widened as her sister held up the makeshift sign: OUT OF ORDER.

"You wouldn't!" Olivia said.

Ivy flashed a devilish smile that said *Wanna bet?* Opening the door a tiny bit, she screwed up her face in concentration and reached around to hang the sign on the doorknob, looking like a safecracker in a heist movie.

"Okay!" Ivy returned, empty-handed. "Make me pink."

"Not pink. *Natural*," Olivia corrected, handing her sister a facial wipe. "Start by taking off your eyeliner."

In a matter of seconds, the white towelette was blacker than the rag Olivia's dad used to shine his shoes. "Oh, my gosh, I knew you wore a lot of eyeliner. But this is really—"

Ivy gave her a look.

"Impressive," Olivia finished and quickly changed the subject. "Anyway, I can't believe how white your regular skin tone is," she said, shaking the can of spray-on tan.

Ivy grabbed her wrist. "You are *not* putting that on my face."

Olivia sighed and looked her sister in the eye. "Ivy, *natural* means healthy. It means aglow with life, awash in sunlight. It means you woke up this morning on the beach in California with a hottie feeding you grapes. You *need* spray-on tan."

"Brendan Daniels doesn't like grapes," Ivy countered frostily. "I know for a fact."

"Well, this washes off anyway," Olivia reassured her sister. "And who's Brendan Daniels?"

Ivy just rolled her eyes. "Spray away." She sighed, closing her eyes and relaxing her face.

After the spray-on tan, Olivia did Ivy's blush and lip gloss. It was the eyeshadow that really clinched it, though. Ivy now actually looked like a living person. Olivia ran some gel through her sister's hair and pulled it back in a ponytail.

"Okay." She smiled, stepping back and admiring her work. "Let's switch clothes." She and Ivy each took a stall. Olivia pulled off her shirt and skirt, folded them neatly, and slipped them underneath the blue metal divider. In return, Ivy passed her a tangled wad of black fabric.

A minute later, Olivia opened the stall door and stood looking at herself in the mirror. A floor-length, black lace skirt was *so* not her style. Then again, she did like the way it was slit up the side.

Actually, she'd like to try it with her green silk top and a pair of black heels.

Suddenly, the stall door beside her opened. Olivia watched her sister take in their reflections. Ivy's eyes shifted back and forth—Olivia wondered for a moment whether Ivy was having trouble remembering which reflection was her own—before settling on the girl in the denim skirt and the pink wrap top.

"Pretty awesome, huh?" Olivia said.

A totally horrified look spread over Ivy's face. "I never thought I'd look like . . ." she began hoarsely.

Uh-oh, Olivia thought.

"Charlotte Brown!" Ivy's face burst into a smile.

"Shut up!" Olivia cried. "I do *not* look like Charlotte Brown!" She threw a cosmetic sponge at her sister's head in mock anger, but Ivy batted it away just in time.

"I don't know—this top is seriously pink," Ivy teased.

"I have *way* better fashion sense than her, and you know it!" Olivia protested lightly.

"Okay, okay, don't pop a blood vessel!" Ivy giggled, holding out her arms for Olivia to spray them with tan, too. Then she took the can and sprayed her lower legs and feet herself. "Geez, how do you wear short skirts like this all the time? I feel as naked as Principal Whitehead's head."

"Well, you look great. Except for the combat boots. They sort of ruin it." Olivia stuck her tongue out at Ivy.

Ivy stuck her tongue out right back.

They traded shoes.

"It's lucky I didn't paint my toenails black," Ivy said, peering down at Olivia's sparkly pink flip-flops.

Olivia finished lacing up the heavy black boots and tried taking a few steps. "Oh, my gosh." She shook her head. "It's like wearing cement blocks!"

Ivy shrugged. "You never know when you might drop a refrigerator on your foot."

Olivia paced back and forth, trying to get the hang of walking. "Okay," she said as she went. "Show me your best cheerleader hair flip."

Ivy turned her head sharply. The dark ponytail

whipped around and smacked her in the face. "Ow!"

"Not that way," Olivia instructed. "Do it with grace. Lead with your chin. Like, just pretend like you're watching a mouse running across the floor with the corner of your eye. That's better. Good. Now let me see you smile." Ivy bared her teeth. "You look like you're about to eat me for dinner." Olivia giggled. "Relax!"

Ivy tried again. And again. "Okay," Olivia said, satisfied. "Whatever you do, don't stop smiling. My sunny disposition is one of my best qualities."

Ivy's face lit up. "You bet!" She bounced, giving a big thumbs-up.

"Don't overdo it," Olivia said. "In fact, you should probably just limit your conversation to 'Really?' 'Really' is like the most versatile word in the English language."

Ivy widened her eyes. "Really?"

Olivia tried not to smile. "Oh, you're going to make me look like a regular Einstein. I can tell."

Ivy beamed. "Really?"

Olivia tried to ignore her. "The other thing you have to remember is that I'm the new girl.

So you can't talk about anything I shouldn't know. If you get stuck, just ask about the latest . . . the latest . . . *whatever*."

Ivy took a deep breath. *"Really?"*

"ENOUGH!" Olivia cried.

Ivy slouched back to her normal self. "My turn!" she sang, picking up her shiny black purse and turning it upside down over the counter. A jumbled waterfall of stuff clattered out: cosmetics, pens, chewing gum, scraps of paper, nail files, pictures, paper clips. Ivy shook the bag. A full-size stapler crashed to the counter. She shook it again. Out tumbled a small, black aerosol can, which Ivy snatched up and displayed in the palm of her hand.

"'Pale Beauty, the spray-on whitener,'" She caressed the can like a model on a TV commercial. "'For that extraspecial made-of-marble look!'"

"You're kidding!" Olivia said. She grabbed the can and inspected the label.

"Lots of Goths use it," Ivy explained, "especially if they're not blessed with a flawless white complexion like mine. Now close your eyes."

Olivia did as she was told. The spray was cool and moist on her skin, but it dried almost instantly. She glanced in the mirror. "I look like a clown!" she said.

"Careful what you say or I'll take your eye out," said Ivy, already leaning in with an eyeliner pencil as fat as a Sharpie marker.

Olivia tried to hold still. She focused on a brown spot on the ceiling and asked, "So what should I talk to your friends about?"

"Excuse me?" Ivy stopped mid upper-left lid. "You cannot talk to my friends. *At all*. Charlotte Brown's one thing. But Sophia Hewitt has been my best friend since we were four years old. She'd be able to tell you weren't me *instantly*."

Olivia knew Ivy was right, but she was still disappointed. "I was sort of excited to be all gloomy," she said, pouting.

"Sorry," Ivy said with genuine sympathy. "What about hiding out in the library? That's where I normally work on my articles for the paper."

"It won't be as fun as gabbing with Goths, but I guess it'll have to do," Olivia conceded. "Luckily,

I have an apple and some health chips to keep me company."

As Ivy finished Olivia's eyes, she said, "Let's meet back here right after lunch and—"

The bell rang.

"Oh, my gosh!" Olivia squealed. "It's time. You have to go!" She scooped up her cosmetics, dumped them back in her pink purse, and handed it to Ivy. "I'll refill your bag once you've gone," she added.

Ivy rested her hands on Olivia's shoulders and looked her right in the eye. "Don't smile too much and don't speak," she said, and Olivia felt her sister pressing her down toward the ground. "And, whatever you do, *please* don't bounce!"

Olivia nodded seriously. She hugged her sister for luck. Then Ivy plastered her face in a smile and headed out the door, clutching Olivia's purse.

Olivia did her best not to grin after her. After all, she was a Goth now.

* 🦇 *

Ivy pushed open the doors to the cafeteria, curling her toes so that Olivia's flip-flops wouldn't fly off her feet.

She tried bouncing as she walked, but then she realized she wasn't smiling. She started smiling, but then she forgot to bounce.

Ivy caught a glimpse of Charlotte Brown and her minions already at their table, and she ducked nervously into the food line.

As the line crept along, Ivy decided to try a hair flip. She thought of a mouse running along the floor, just as Olivia said, and followed it out of the corner of her eye. Her ponytail swung around smoothly. Then the mouse ran under Charlotte Brown's chair. Ivy imagined Charlotte jumping up and down, screaming her head off.

There. That was better. Now it was suddenly easy to smile and bounce.

"A burger, please!" Ivy requested perkily when it was her turn.

Her full tray in hand, Ivy set her sights on the Table of Evil. Charlotte saw her and waved excitedly, then rested her hand meaningfully on the shoulder of the boy next to her—none other than Jeff Moore, the original beefy superbunny. Even from this far away, Ivy could see Charlotte fluttering her eyelashes.

Ivy made her way across the cafeteria bouncily. She was almost at the Table of Evil when she realized with a jolt that she was walking right past her usual table, where all her friends were eating lunch. She nearly tripped over one of her flip-flops and had to bend down to get it back on.

Sophia was saying, "It's seriously the most important night of the whole year" to Holly.

What am I doing? Ivy thought nervously.

As Ivy straightened, Charlotte caught her eye again and mouthed, *"Isn't he hot?"* She was leaning toward Jeff like she was hanging on his every word.

I remember, thought Ivy, turning her smile back on. *I'm getting back at Charlotte Brown.*

She plopped her tray down across from Charlotte and Jeff and unleashed an exuberant, "Hi, guys!" *Oops,* she thought. *I wasn't supposed to overdo it.*

Fortunately, Katie and Allison didn't seem to notice. "Hi, Olivia!" they replied.

Then Charlotte said, "What do you think you're doing?"

Ivy's heart stopped. "Uh . . . I'm, like," she stammered, "having . . . lunch?"

54

Charlotte blinked in disbelief. "Since when," she asked wide-eyed, "do self-respecting cheer-leaders eat hamburgers for lunch?"

Allison and Katie nodded in concern.

"Yes, well, you are so totally right," Ivy said, her heart beating again. "And I don't know what came over me, but I just really wanted a burger today."

"I think it's cool," said Jeff Moore, smiling broadly at Ivy from beneath his crew cut. "Refreshing, actually. A girl who really eats. All the girls I know won't even have a French fry unless it's covered in fatless dressing."

"I love hamburgers!" Charlotte said quickly. "Just not from the cafeteria." She giggled uncom-fortably. "Anyway, let me introduce you. Olivia, this is Jeff. Remember I was telling you about him? Jeff's co-captain of the Devils football team."

"Really?" Ivy said in wide-eyed wonder as she took a bite of her burger.

"Plus he's all-state cross-country," Charlotte continued, savoring the words like she was eating a chocolate.

"Baseball, too," Jeff added.

"You should see him in uniform." Charlotte winked.

"Rea-lly," Ivy said with a knowing smile. Jeff chomped a French fry.

Ivy wasn't about to stop now. "So, what's the latest in Devils football?"

"I scored seventy-two touchdowns last year." Jeff swallowed. "It was a county record. This year, I'm going for eighty."

"Really?" Ivy said automatically.

"Yeah." He cocked his head. "Hey, Charlotte tells me you're trying out for the cheerleading squad."

Ivy nodded coyly.

"She says you're pretty good," said Jeff.

"For a new girl," Charlotte put in.

"You sure *look* like you'd be a good cheerleader," said Jeff, with what he obviously thought was a winning smile.

I've sunk to a new low, Ivy thought. *Jockstrap Jeff Moore likes me!*

The look on Charlotte Brown's face made it seriously worth it, though. "Jeff!" she said, clutching at his arm like she was drowning. "Oh, my gosh, Jeff. We forgot wrestling!"

"Oh, yeah," Jeff nodded, looking impressed. "I wrestle, too."

Charlotte narrowed her eyes. Then she reached over, grabbed the last bite of Ivy's burger off her plate, and dramatically popped it in her mouth, smiling at Jeff goofily as she chewed.

Katie and Allison looked seriously shocked.

This is going better than I ever imagined! Ivy thought, wiggling her toes in delight underneath the table. *Charlotte Brown is literally eating her words!*

* 🐰 *

Olivia was having a great time trudging back toward the science hall bathroom at the end of lunch period. Now that she was used to Ivy's boots, every step made her feel really powerful, like she could march through a crowd of people and they would all move out of her way. Her mouth set firmly, she peered out at people from behind a wall of hair. A passing Goth girl murmured, "Hi, Ivy."

"Hi," Olivia answered without stopping. She tried not to let a tiny smile escape, but she couldn't help it. *Being a Goth is so cool!* she thought.

Her period in the library had flown by. At first, Olivia had been annoyed that she'd forgotten to bring *Thrice Bitten*, the latest Count Vira book, with her. But then she'd remembered reading about an old French short story that, according to what she'd seen on a vampire fiction fansite, was one of the first vampire stories ever written. She'd decided to see if they had it.

"*The Horla and Other Stories of Guy de Maupassant.* It looks like this isn't the first time you've checked this book out, Ivy," the librarian had said when she'd looked at the computer screen.

Olivia had shrugged as she'd thought Ivy might, taken the book, and started reading. . . .

The story had been so awesome that, before Olivia knew it, the bell had rung for the end of the period. Now she was in a hurry to get back to the bathroom and find out from Ivy how things had gone with Charlotte Brown.

Olivia rounded the corner and crashed right

into a Goth boy! Her book flew from her hands and skittered across the floor.

She looked at the boy as he bent to pick up her book. He was thin with broad shoulders, wearing black cargo pants and a black button-down work shirt. His pale face was surrounded by dark disheveled curls. He looked familiar, probably from one of her classes.

"Are you okay?" he asked, sounding concerned.

"I'm fine," Olivia said. "Sorry. I guess my boots got ahead of me."

The boy handed Olivia her book, and she finally figured out which subject they had together. "I know you," she said with a nod. "You're in my social studies class."

The boy gave her a weird look. He frowned, looking cute, if you were into the brooding type. "Ivy," he said slowly, "we've been in the same social studies class for the last three years."

"Uh . . ." Olivia fumbled. "Of course. Just kidding?" She tried to grimace in a friendly way.

He glanced at the cover of her book. "Looks interesting," he said, holding it out to her.

She knew she should just take the book and

go, but it really was something that more people should read. "It is. *The Horla*'s about this guy who thinks he's being stalked by a vampire. It, uh, really sucks."

"Yeah?" the boy said, clearly intrigued.

"Yeah. It's all told in diary entries, and this guy doesn't know if he's going crazy or what," explained Olivia.

He nodded. "I'll have to read it."

"You should," she said. Then she spotted Ivy down the hallway. *Gosh, she really does look fabulous in that skirt!* Olivia thought.

The boy was still looking at her. "What else do you like to read?"

Over his shoulder, Olivia saw Ivy stop and stare at her, mouth agape, looking completely panicked.

Oh, no, thought Olivia. *Lunch with Charlotte was a bust!*

Ivy stamped her flip-flop on the ground and frantically motioned for Olivia to follow her into the bathroom *right now*! Olivia mumbled, "Gotta go," to the Goth boy and rushed away. She heard him call, "Hey, Ivy!" as she pushed through the bathroom door.

"Oh, my gosh, what happened?" Olivia cried when she saw her sister's stricken look in the bathroom mirror.

"How the heck am I supposed to know what happened?" Ivy demanded with a wild look in her eyes. "That's what I should be asking you. WHAT HAPPENED?" She washed the spray-on tan off her face, arms, and legs, pulled her hair out of its ponytail, and abruptly disappeared into a stall to change.

Wow! Olivia thought as she washed off the heavy eyeliner and white makeup. *Lunch must have been really awful.*

"I'm really sorry, Ivy," Olivia said, taking the next stall and unlacing her boots. "You were right. It was a bad idea. Charlotte was never going to fall for it."

"Charlotte?" Ivy's voice rang off the bathroom walls. "Charlotte fell for it like a skydiver without a parachute. I'm not talking about Charlotte. I'm talking about *Brendan Daniels*!"

"But I thought you were having lunch with Jeff Moore," Olivia said to the blue metal divider.

"I am going to *strangle* you," Ivy said, clearly

exasperated. Olivia's clothes appeared at ankle level.

"You mean the guy in the hallway?" Olivia asked, gradually piecing things together as she handed back Ivy's clothes.

"Yes!" Ivy said.

"You don't like him?" Olivia guessed.

"No!" Ivy cried. "I am *utterly* in love with him!"

"Oh." It all made total sense now. Olivia felt like such a dork. "I get it," she said sheepishly.

"Well?" Ivy prompted. "What did he say?"

"I bumped into him by accident," Olivia explained. "He asked about my book. It's due back next Tuesday, by the way."

"Did he . . ." Ivy's voice was suddenly much quieter. "Did he know my name?" Olivia heard her sister emerge from the next stall.

Olivia straightened her skirt and pushed open her own door. "You mean you've never even spoken to him?" she asked.

Ivy sighed dramatically and shut her eyes. "No."

"Well," said Olivia brightly. "It appears your

unusual mating strategy worked, because I'm pretty sure the guy is totally into you."

Ivy's eyes flew open. "What? What did he say?"

"Nothing. He just . . . he seemed like he really wanted to talk to you. He was, like, hanging on my every word. He didn't want me—*you*—to walk away."

"Like how?" Ivy demanded.

"Stop obsessing," Olivia said, handing Ivy her bag and taking back her own purse. "If I were you, I'd thank me for breaking the ice."

"I told you not to talk to anyone!" Ivy protested.

"Come on," Olivia said, giving her sister a playful poke in the arm. "Will you please just tell me what happened with Charlotte?"

Ivy leaned back against the bathroom counter to lace up her boots. "Well," she said matter-of-factly. "It's safe to say you're not the only matchmaker in this bathroom. In fact, lunch went so well that Jeff Moore asked you to go to the mall with him after school."

Olivia's jaw dropped. "No!"

"Oh, yes," said Ivy as she reapplied her makeup and a little sunblock. "I said you were busy of course. He's too dumb for you. But you should have seen the look on Charlotte's face!" She did a perfect imitation: chest out, mouth open, eyes popping out of her head. Olivia laughed.

"Still," said Ivy, letting her hair fall in front of her face. "I'm glad to be myself again. Talking about sports makes the lunch period seem *eternal*."

"Careful," Olivia said as she pulled out the container of facial wipes. "Brendan might like sports."

"Why?" Ivy gasped. "What'd he say about sports?"

CHAPTER 5

"All right," said Ivy, looking in the mirror one last time. "Swear to me that I don't have any more of that stuff on my face." She couldn't imagine anything more devastating than Brendan Daniels seeing her and noticing that her ear was all brown.

"I swear," replied Olivia. "You look totally pale and ill again."

"Good," Ivy said gratefully. "Almost ready?"

Olivia wrinkled her nose. "I still have to fix my hair. Besides, maybe it's better if we leave separately. Won't people get suspicious if we're seen together too much?"

Ivy nodded. "You're right. I'll go first."

Olivia put down her lip gloss. "You know," she said, "you really did look terrific in that skirt."

"What I know," said Ivy, hugging her sister, "is that *you* look terrific in that skirt. See you in science."

Ivy pulled open the heavy door.

"Ciao," Olivia called after her.

With a shock, Ivy saw Brendan Daniels less than ten lockers away. He looked like he was waiting for someone.

He must have been there this whole time! Ivy realized, her heart jumping around in her chest like a bat caught in daylight. *What if he heard what we were saying?*

"Ivy," he called.

He's talking to me!

"Ivy," he repeated, coming closer.

Ivy forced herself to put one boot in front of the other. She ran a hand along the wall of lockers to steady herself. "Hi, Brendan," she said in a tiny voice.

"Listen," he began. He was the most beautiful boy she had ever seen. "Do you . . ." He stopped and looked at the floor.

She heard her voice say, "Uh-huh?"

He looked right at her. Ivy put both hands on her bag to keep them from shaking.

"Do you want to meet up at the mall? Like, after school?" he finally asked.

Ivy didn't respond. She thought she must have misheard him.

"Hey, listen, I . . . never mind," Brendan gabbled. He shook his head. "I'll see you around." Suddenly he was walking away.

Speak! the voice in Ivy's head cried. *Speak!*

"Brendan!" Ivy croaked. He spun around. "Um, what time?" she asked.

His smile shone. "Does four work for you?"

"Sure," she answered, trying to sound relaxed. "I'll tell my dad I'll be home before sundown."

"Great," he said. He held up his hand, and then was gone.

Ivy collapsed against the lockers. Her hands were still shaking, and her heart pounded. People looked at her as they walked by on their way to class, but she didn't care.

Well, she thought breathlessly, *that's one good thing about having a twin sister who's a social butterfly!*

As if on cue, Olivia emerged from the bathroom. "Wow! You look like you just did a triple handspring and landed on your head," Olivia said. "What happened?"

"He asked me out," Ivy whispered. She couldn't believe she was saying it.

"What?" Olivia asked, drawing closer. "Talk louder."

"He asked me out!" Ivy said again hoarsely.

Olivia's face burst into a smile. "Go, Ivy!" she shouted really loudly.

"Shut *up*!" Ivy scolded, even though she couldn't help smiling, too.

"That's awesome!" Olivia said. "When's the big date?"

"Today. After school." Ivy panted. "The mall."

Olivia gave her a squeeze. "I have to scoot or I'm going to be late for art, but we are going to have *so* much to talk about in science!" She hurried off with a wink.

Ivy was going to be late for class, too. She worked up the strength to start walking, and, as she made her way slowly through the prebell crowd, she let herself imagine her coming date with Brendan.

They would walk around Spins, the record store, together; she knew he was into punk. He'd hold up a pair of black jeans at Dungeon Clothing. He'd sit across from her in the food court, drinking red lemonade through a straw.

As Ivy turned into the main hallway, she imagined the two of them walking side by side, talking on and on about . . .

What are we going to talk about? she thought with a jolt.

Her wave of excitement disappeared like predawn fog. How was she going to talk to Brendan Daniels for a whole afternoon when five minutes ago she could barely string two words together?

She imagined herself with Brendan at the mall again, but now she couldn't picture him smiling. They'd sit in silence. He'd have to order another red lemonade and drink it just to kill time. He would think she was an utter loser. She'd try to come up with something funny to say, probably some stupid joke about the school paper, but he wouldn't laugh. He'd just look away.

I can't go, Ivy thought.

The bell for the next class rang.

I'll tell him I'm sick, she decided.

Suddenly somebody came up from behind and linked arms with her. She nearly jumped out of her skin.

"And where were *you* at lunch today?" Sophia demanded, poking her in the side. "Giddyup! We're late for English."

Ivy didn't say anything. She let Sophia lead the way.

"What's with you?" her friend said. "You look like you've seen a ghost. What, did Brendan Daniels ask you for a pen or something?" she teased.

"I don't feel well," Ivy replied weakly. "I think I'm sick."

Sophia stopped in her tracks. "No way, Ivy." She shook her head. "You are *not* going to bail on me! You promised me ages ago that you would come to today's meeting."

Ivy realized that she had completely forgotten about the meeting. She couldn't go to the mall with Brendan; she'd agreed weeks ago to go to a meeting after school with her best friend. Sophia would put a stake through Ivy if she backed out now.

"I know you, Ivy," Sophia declared. "You *never* get sick!"

"That's not true," Ivy replied halfheartedly. "I got sick in fourth grade."

Sophia smirked. "You got a marble stuck in your ear."

"Okay, okay," Ivy said. She took a deep breath. "I'm going. Four o'clock, right?"

Sophia nodded, and Ivy felt the blood drain from her heart. *It's better this way*, she told herself. *I'll put a note in his locker after school, telling him I can't go.*

She let her hair fall in front of her face and followed her friend into their fourth-period class.

* 🐰 *

"Okay, class!" Mr. Strain shouted, holding a ridiculous red hunting cap on his head. "Spread out! I want to see a full report on this soccer field's flora! Remember, conifers are extra credit!"

Olivia clutched her sweatshirt around her and looked down at the leaf-covered grass. "I'm all in favor of science class outside," she said just loud enough so that Ivy would hear. "But this is really dumb."

She turned to see her sister's reaction, but . . . Ivy was gone. Olivia spun around and spotted her sister's black figure trudging off into the distance. "Wait up!" Olivia shouted.

She caught up with Ivy near the edge of the field. "Hey!" she said. "What are—"

Ivy held up a red leaf. "Do you think this is an oak or an ash?" she asked tentatively.

"An oak," Olivia told her, slightly confused. "I didn't know where you went."

Ivy threw the leaf away and bent down to pick up another and then another. She mumbled, "I didn't want anyone to disturb my leaf sampling."

"Okaaay," said Olivia doubtfully.

Ivy kept working silently, picking up leaves, looking at them, jotting notes down, throwing them back. She looked really sad.

Olivia sighed. She touched her sister's shoulder. "You're really nervous about your date with Brendan, huh?"

Ivy moved away.

"It's okay, Ivy," Olivia continued, full of sympathy. "This summer, there was this guy I had the biggest crush on and he—"

"I'm not going," Ivy said to the grass.

"What?" Olivia said.

"I can't." Ivy shook her head. "I forgot I had this meeting I have to go to. I promised Sophia ages ago."

"The guy you're 'utterly in love with' asked you out, and you're *not going?*" Olivia cried.

Ivy wouldn't look at her. "That's right," she said. "And it's for the best anyway. If I go, I know I'd just do something seriously grave, like throw up on him on the escalator or something. And then I'd regret it for the rest of eternity."

"What are you *talking* about?" Olivia demanded.

"I know I would, Olivia," Ivy barreled on. She was scattering leaves this way and that. "And he'll hate me—worse, he'll think I'm seriously bizarre. And—and I'll have ruined everything."

"Oh, my gosh," Olivia said with a shake of her head. "If this were the movies, I'd have to slap your face to make you snap out of it." She

73

was so dumbfounded she couldn't think of anything else to say. Finally she just sat down on the ground, eyes closed, thinking hard. She could hear her sister scribbling and picking up leaves.

It was a windy day, and Olivia shivered. She wished she was still wearing Ivy's long skirt. *That's it!* she thought, springing to her feet and rushing to her sister's side.

"I really wish you'd stop disturbing my sample," Ivy said, stomping around.

Olivia grabbed her sister by the shoulders. "Ivy, we have to switch again," she said sternly.

"You're right," Ivy replied with a frown. "You'd be much better on a date."

"No, *you'll* go on the date," Olivia said, grinning. "I'll go to the meeting!"

"Oh!" Ivy said, sounding shocked. Then she shook her head. "I think it's one of those meetings where a cheerleader might stick out, though."

Ivy was clearly confused, so Olivia had no choice but to speak extra slowly. "There will be two Ivy's, you dork," she explained. "Impostor Ivy—that's me—will go to the meeting with

Sophia. Real Ivy—that's you—will go to the mall with Brendan."

Ivy silently studied the leaf in her hands for a long moment. Finally, she looked up. "I know you're trying to help, Olivia." She sighed. "But it won't work. This meeting will be all Goths. And even if you could get by everyone else, you'll never make it past Sophia."

"If you can fool Charlotte, I can fool Sophia," said Olivia confidently.

"She's my oldest friend," countered Ivy.

"Don't underestimate me," Olivia pleaded. "Just because I'm a cheerleader that doesn't mean I don't know all about Goths. I'm like the number one vampire novel fan in middle school today. I've read every Count Vira book four times. I promise, I'll fit right in."

Ivy laughed uncomfortably.

"All right, class," Mr. Strain's voice wafted across the field. "Time's almost up!"

"Say you'll do it," Olivia said intently.

"I want to, Olivia. But . . ."

Olivia took her hands. "Ivy, I swear to you as your twin sister that if you don't go on this date,

75

you will never forgive yourself. The boy you like likes you. He likes *you*. The only thing that will definitely ruin that is if you blow him off."

"But what will we talk about?" Ivy asked desperately. "Somehow I don't think asking about the 'latest' is going to work in this situation."

"I'll help you," Olivia said firmly. She was not going to take no for an answer. "You'll be fine, just like you were at lunch."

Ivy was silent.

"Girls!" Mr. Strain called.

"Say you'll do it," Olivia whispered. *"Please."*

Ivy blinked. "Okay," she said, a smile creeping onto her face as she squeezed Olivia's hand. "But *I* get to wear my black velvet sneakers."

★ 🦇 ★

Olivia used Ivy's cell phone to call her mother as soon as the final bell rang, and told her that she was going to Ivy's house after school. This was technically true, because twenty minutes later, Olivia stood with Ivy at the base of a willow tree–lined driveway that led up a small hill. At the top was a house that looked like something out of *Gone with the Wind*. It had windows that were about fifteen feet tall and a columned front porch that spanned the front of the house.

Ivy started up the drive.

"This is your house?" said Olivia. She thought of the two-story brick house her family had just moved into on the other side of Franklin Grove. Olivia really liked their new house—her bedroom was at least twice the size of her old one—but this place was a total mansion.

"Yeah," Ivy said. "Why?"

"It's nice," said Olivia, shaking gravel out of one of her flip-flops.

They hustled up the hill and climbed the sweeping front steps. A huge lantern of dark red glass hung above the porch, flickering even though it was day. Ivy paused before turning the burnished brass knob on the ornately carved oak front door. "Stay here for a sec." She disappeared inside.

From where she stood beside a pile of firewood taller than she was, Olivia could see almost all Franklin Grove below her. It looked beautiful with houses poking up among the trees. She spotted the roof of the school in the distance.

Ivy reappeared. "Come on," she said, pulling Olivia inside. "My dad's not home."

Olivia's eyes slowly adjusted to the dim light. The entryway was huge, with walls covered in interlocking patterns of stone and dark mahogany. She could just make out an extravagant staircase snaking up to the second floor; a window above it was shrouded by thick dark velvet curtains.

Apparently, Ivy's not the only black sheep in her family, Olivia thought. *This place is Goth heaven!*

Olivia followed her sister past a suit of armor and down a twisting flight of stone steps. A series of electric candelabra lit the way. They came to a landing and turned a corner.

Suddenly Olivia found herself at the top of a staircase. To her left was a window covered with a heavy velvet curtain, which Olivia realized must be set just above ground level. As she followed Ivy down the stairs, the wall to her right fell away to offer a clear view of the spacious basement room below.

In the center of the stone floor was a huge, round, cream-colored rug. Tall mahogany shelves crammed with papers and books took up the far wall. In one corner was a huge desk with a computer and toppling stacks of CDs; in another was a big black bed strewn with funky pillows. Black shoes littered the floor everywhere, looking like fallen bats. "This is the coolest room I have ever seen!" Olivia admitted as she reached the bottom.

"Thank you," said Ivy, sounding pleased.

Olivia turned around and noticed some words written in big black calligraphy on the stones that ran down the side of the stairway: "The matter is that I never get any rest, and my nights devour my days."

"That is so weird," she murmured. "That's from the Guy de Maupassant story I read in the library today. I even told Brendan to read it!"

"*The Horla*?" Ivy responded. "It sucks, doesn't it?"

"That's exactly what I told him." Olivia grinned. Then she noticed the largest wardrobe she had ever seen, made of ornately carved mahogany. It had five doors, one of which hung open. Necklaces and purses glimmered in the dim light.

Olivia charged over, flinging open the doors.

There were racks upon racks of sweaters, skirts, tops, and dresses in every imaginable shade of black, purple, sapphire, and claret, with occasional flashes of emerald and gray. There was one section filled with more black shoes and boots.

"I knew we had something in common," Olivia said excitedly as she took inventory.

She immediately pulled out a long-sleeved, lightweight, V-necked top in a rich wine red with slashed sleeves. "Can I try this on?" she asked.

★ 🦇 ★

Ivy stood looking in the mirror, examining the outfit her sister had helped her choose for her first date with Brendan. She hadn't worn this sweater in ages, but she had to admit that Olivia was right—she looked drop-dead in it. Olivia had also picked out a formfitting, long black skirt that Ivy hadn't even known she owned.

"What do you think of this?" Olivia said behind her, referring to her latest creation. She was wearing a black baby tee that said KILL ME SOFTLY in gray Gothic letters and a black chiffon-and-velvet-striped skirt. It must have been the sixth outfit she'd tried.

"Now *that*," said Ivy, "looks like me."

Olivia inspected herself in the mirror. "Let's accessorize," she decided.

She went down to the end of the wardrobe and came back with an armful of jangly, strappy things. She carefully handed Ivy some silver bangles and a pair of big silver hoop earrings, saying, "I can't believe you wear clip-ons," to which Ivy just shrugged. For herself, she'd chosen a black velvet choker.

Ivy sprayed some Pale Beauty on Olivia's face, and then they crowded side by side in the mirror to finish their makeup. They both chose the same dark maroon lipstick.

Ivy glanced at her chunky watch and shot her sister a pained look. "You have to meet Sophia at school in fifteen minutes, and I still don't know what I'm supposed to talk to Brendan about."

"Okay," Olivia said, hurrying to finish applying her eyeliner. "Want to know the secret to an awesome first date?"

Ivy nodded impatiently.

"Ask questions. Get him to talk about himself: his family, his friends, what *he* likes."

Ivy thought, *That's it?* and looked at Olivia skeptically.

"It's all about getting to know each other," explained Olivia. "And, if he's really boyfriend material, he'll ask you some questions, too."

Ivy got nervous. "What will I do if that happens?"

"Talk. Tell the truth. Tell him about what you like and what drives you crazy. The only thing you might want to leave out is your brand-new, cheerleading twin sister. That might freak him out."

"No kidding," Ivy said, rolling her eyes. "That should be the number one rule of romance: no secret twin sister revelations until at least the third date."

Olivia giggled and stuffed her clothes into Ivy's fuzzy black backpack. "And remember," she said, slinging on the bag, "even if you're not the perky fashion victim, you could try smiling once or twice."

Ivy heard a door slam upstairs. "My dad's home." She winced. "And I don't think now's really the right time to introduce you to him. No offense."

"I'm not going to tell my parents about you either," said Olivia, "at least not before we figure a few things out for ourselves."

Ivy nodded. "We'd better sneak out the window," she said. She led Olivia up the staircase and threw aside the curtain.

"This is so secret agent." Olivia giggled as Ivy pushed her out into the backyard.

A minute later, they'd reached the bottom of the driveway. "So what's this meeting I'm going to?" Olivia asked.

"I'm not completely sure," admitted Ivy. "Sophia is constantly signing me up for clubs and stuff. I think she didn't want to tell me, because she knew I wouldn't like it."

They took the shortcut through the woods behind a neighbor's house.

"Whatever you do," Ivy instructed as they marched down the leaf-covered path, "don't look happy to be there. No perkiness, no enthusiasm, no 'Hi, guys!' You do any of that, and they'll eat you alive."

"Got it. Where's the meeting going to be?"

"I'm not sure. I know it's not at school though.

It will probably just be a bunch of"—Ivy hesitated—"Goths debating something."

Suddenly Ivy started to have second thoughts. *What if somebody says something that makes Olivia suspicious?* She stopped at a fork in the path. "Anyway," she said nervously, "don't pay too much attention to anything anyone says. At all."

Olivia looked at her in confusion.

"You know, b-because," Ivy stammered, "Goths can have really strange . . . uh . . . senses of humor."

"Okay," Olivia said, and shrugged.

"I'm going this way to the mall." Ivy gestured down one path. "Keep going straight, and you'll end up back on the field behind school. You're meeting Sophia by the front doors."

They hugged. "You're going to be irresistible!" said Olivia.

"Don't do anything I wouldn't do," Ivy answered. "Seriously." Then she hurried off down the path to the mall, determined not to throw up at any point during her first date with Brendan Daniels—even on the escalator.

CHAPTER 6

Bring on the Goths! thought Olivia.

"You're late," said Sophia, charging up with her black scarf swinging. "I've been out of the photo lab for twenty minutes already. You weren't trying to back out on me, were you?"

"No," said Olivia, making sure she didn't bounce. "I just ran home to change. And I couldn't find my"—she hesitated and Sophia peered at her skeptically—"my fuzzy backpack," Olivia finished.

Sophia's mouth dropped open. "You mean *my* fuzzy backpack that you borrowed and never returned!"

Oops. "I guess that's the one," Olivia said hoarsely.

"Well," said Sophia, "it *is* a killer fashion statement. You look deadly."

"Thank you," said Olivia.

"So let's *go*." Sophia pushed her toward the sidewalk. "I don't want to be late!"

So far, so good, Olivia thought with a rush of relief. If she could make it to the meeting without arousing Sophia's suspicions, everything else would be easy.

They cut across the school parking lot and turned onto Thornhill Road. Olivia glanced over and caught Sophia sneaking a sideways look at her.

Shoot, Olivia thought. *She's onto me.*

Sophia stopped and grabbed her arm. "We need to talk," she said seriously.

Olivia held her breath and waited for the ax to fall.

"Listen, I know you're not going to enjoy this," Sophia said, frowning. "In fact, you're going to hate it. But I *really* want to be on the planning committee."

Olivia let herself breathe again. It seemed Sophia hadn't discovered her secret—yet! And Olivia had been head of the planning committee for the spring carnival at her old school. It rocked. "Planning committee for what?" she asked curiously.

"The All Hallows' Ball," Sophia said apologetically. She sounded like a little kid who knows she's in trouble. "Every year, they use the same lifeless professional photographer with a comb-over, and I think I could do something seriously great and candid. But we have to be on the planning committee first."

Olivia blurted, "That sounds cool."

Sophia looked completely shocked, and Olivia realized that Ivy would *not* think party planning was cool. *At all*.

"I mean you taking the pictures sounds cool. *Not* party planning," Olivia added hastily. Then she continued in a glum tone, meant to convey Goth resignation, "Just don't expect me to say anything in this meeting. I'll sit there, but that's it."

"Agreed," Sophia said, looking relieved. "Thanks, Ivy."

As they walked, Olivia wondered why she hadn't heard anything about the ball before. At her old school, there would have been posters everywhere.

The tree-lined street had turned into a concrete thoroughfare, and they walked past a Funky Chicken and a Marly's Discount Superstore. Sophia leaped up on a bench and tiptoed along it, jumping down. Olivia struggled to limit her reaction to a close-lipped Goth smile, but it wasn't easy. Then she noticed Sophia's earrings—two little black bowling balls with white bowling pins dangling below them.

"Your earrings are so cute!" Olivia exclaimed.

"Don't be such a witch," Sophia replied drily. She must have thought her friend was being sarcastic.

Olivia mentally kicked herself. She *had* to stop using words like "cute," or she'd never make it through the afternoon in one piece.

Sophia veered into the parking lot of a giant FoodMart. Olivia was a little surprised, considering they were already running late, but she followed Ivy's friend inside without comment.

Maybe they were supposed to bring food to the meeting, like pretzels or something.

But Sophia didn't even go to the snack aisle. Olivia followed her past paper towels and laundry detergent to the back of the store. They stopped in front of a scruffy stock boy with jet-black hair and a nose ring, who was stacking cases of cranberry juice on a cart.

Out of nowhere, Sophia said, "Pumpernickel."

Well, that's a lame meeting snack, thought Olivia.

Without even looking at them, the boy silently pulled a key from a chain that hung from his belt loop and unlocked a gray door marked STAFF ONLY.

Sophia walked through, and Olivia hustled after her.

This is weird, thought Olivia.

They started down an impossibly steep, dimly lit staircase. There was no handrail, and Olivia was scared she'd trip over her boots. Sophia barreled down fearlessly ahead of her.

Clearly this thing was a total secret, Olivia decided. But what kind of dance required a hush-hush meeting in the basement of a supermarket?

The only thing Olivia could think of was a TV special she'd seen about some girls in Europe who threw massive raves in warehouses. All their planning was top secret because the cops were always trying to bust them.

My mom will never *let me go to this dance*, thought Olivia with a tinge of disappointment.

The stairs led to a long, narrow hallway. The girls passed an unmarked door, behind which Olivia could have sworn a crowd of people was laughing and talking. Finally, after squeezing past a stack of chairs, they reached the end of the hall and another nondescript door.

Sophia pushed it open, and Olivia was surprised to find herself in a room that looked a lot like the conference room at her dad's old office: dry-erase board, pukey beige carpet, black imitation-leather office chairs. The only real difference was the huge round stone table in the center of the room.

There were some Goths standing around drinking cherry punch. A serious-looking girl with chunky glasses was organizing papers on the table.

"Hi, Soph," said a girl wearing a studded collar.

She nodded at Olivia. "Hey, Ivy. I can't believe you actually came."

Olivia had no idea what the girl's name was. She shifted uncomfortably.

Luckily, the girl in the chunky glasses cleared her throat in an official way and bailed Olivia out by saying, "We're five minutes late. Let's get started."

Olivia was already lowering herself into a seat when she noticed that everyone else was simply standing behind their chairs. She jerked herself back up.

The room was silent. The girl in charge held her hands above the table like she was warming them over a fire and closed her eyes. "May the Secret be cloaked in darkness," she said solemnly.

"And never see light of day," the group responded as one.

Olivia was baffled. *This must be the weird sense of humor Ivy was talking about,* she thought. She hoped no one had noticed that she hadn't joined in. They were now all sitting down, so she quickly slipped into her chair.

"Okay, people," the girl began. "We only have

three weeks to pull off Franklin Grove's two hundred and second annual All Hallows' Ball, and I'm determined to make it the best one ever. This is the first of three planning committee meetings. Today we need to decide on the theme and who's going to be responsible for—"

She was interrupted by raucous laughter in the hallway, and suddenly the door swung open. In slouched four boys with dirty-looking hair and heavy metal T-shirts.

It was the boys who had cornered Olivia in the hall at school, the ones Ivy called the Beasts. Olivia clutched her backpack nervously underneath the table. *It's okay,* she told herself. *Ivy isn't scared of them.*

"What a surprise!" the girl leading the meeting said coolly. "You guys are late."

"Sorry, Melissa," said one Beast sarcastically as he and his friends grabbed seats. "We had to, uh, grab a bite."

The other Beasts guffawed dumbly, but everyone else just groaned.

"You wish," said a girl with a streak of white in her hair.

"As I was saying," Melissa snapped, calling the meeting back to order. "The first thing we need to do is pick a theme. Let's brainstorm."

People started calling out ideas. A boy with a shaved head said, "What about a costume ball?"

"Or a forest party?" suggested the girl with the white streak. "Like where everybody dresses up as trees and things? We could do it in the woods."

"The Ball of the Future?"

"What if everybody had to wear something purple?"

"I once went to a sweet sixteen where there was an ice cream bar, and people were seriously into it."

"I know! What about Franklin Grove Star Search?"

Melissa did not look impressed.

Oh, my gosh, Olivia thought suddenly, *I have the best idea!* "How about a vampire theme?" she blurted. "You could do coffins instead of tables, and spiderwebs and bats hanging everywhere. And . . . ooh, you could even get a big projector and show that old Dracula movie—you know, the black-and-white one with that Bela guy? And someone could take black-and-white photographs of all the guests!"

Nobody spoke for a long time. At last the boy with the shaved head said, "So you want to perpetuate the stereotype?"

Huh? thought Olivia.

"No, Ivy's onto something . . ." Melissa decided, nodding slowly. "Retro is in."

"Can you imagine? Everyone in fangs and capes and stuff?" mused the girl with the streak of white hair. "That would be deadly."

"I agree," said the girl with the studded collar, turning to Olivia. "This idea really sucks, Ivy."

For a second, Olivia thought she might get thrown out of the meeting, but then she remembered again that "suck" was good. She glanced over at Sophia, who was staring at her in shock but who still managed a small, surprised smile.

In the food court at the mall, Ivy fidgeted at a little table, watching as Brendan Daniels waited in line at Deep Slice for a small Carnivore's Delight pizza for the two of them to share. A long silver key chain looped out of his back pocket. He turned and smiled at her from under his cowl of dark curls. She gave a small breathless wave and continued stacking the spice shakers on the table.

Their date so far hadn't gone anything like Ivy had imagined. The first thing Brendan had done was lead her right past Spins and Dungeon Clothing to the arcade, where he challenged her to an air hockey tournament.

For the next forty minutes, they had barely spoken. Instead, they shouted and laughed and banged their little round paddles on the table as the thin puck whizzed between them, cracking against the boards.

Ivy took four games out of seven. "You let me win!" she had said, grinning and bravely nudging Brendan's arm as they walked out of the arcade.

"You think so?" he'd replied, spinning on his heels and grabbing her hand. "Then let's make it best of eleven."

Brendan had won that round, but only just. He'd promised Ivy they'd keep a running tally.

Now she was watching as he filled two huge cups at the drinks dispenser. *When he comes back,* she thought, remembering her sister's advice, *I'm going to ask him about himself.*

Brendan approached carefully, his eyes on the two tall cups that were filled to the brim with red lemonade. Steam rose off the pizza and bathed his face. He set the food down in front of Ivy and looked at her.

"You know I've been scared to death," he said.

"Of spilling something?" Ivy asked, pretending to be distracted by balancing the oregano atop the pepper atop the salt.

Across from her, Brendan shook his head. "I have so many questions I want to ask you," he told her.

Ivy blinked at her tower and prepared to put the crushed red pepper flakes on top. "Like what?"

"I don't know." He shrugged. "Everything?"

Ivy couldn't help recalling what Olivia had said about boys who ask questions. *Boyfriend material!* she thought, her heart pounding. She tried not to seem excited.

Brendan asked, "Do you have any brothers or sisters?"

Ivy's hand jerked, and the chili peppers

96

knocked into the oregano, and the entire tower of spices collapsed, crashing right into Ivy's full cup of lemonade and sending it flying.

Brendan was already on his feet. "Don't worry," he said. "I'll get some napkins."

★ 🐰 ★

Pretty soon everybody at the planning committee meeting was talking about the theme Olivia had suggested for the ball. Meanwhile, the Beasts kept whispering and snickering to one another.

Finally Melissa turned to them and said, "Care to share?"

They all looked up. One of them said, "Uh, yeah. We got an idea."

"Okay," said Melissa.

"It's a really excellent idea for a—what do you call it?—a decoration," the same Beast went on. His friends chuckled.

"Totally excellent," one of them muttered.

"*Okay,*" said Melissa impatiently.

"A blood fountain," the first Beast announced.

"A *what?*" said Melissa.

"You know. A fountain of *blood.*" All the Beasts were totally cracking up now.

"As if," said Melissa, rolling her eyes. "Talk about perpetuating stereotypes. Besides, fountains were last year's party feature."

Sophia whispered, "What losers!" in Olivia's ear, and Olivia felt relieved that Ivy's friends didn't want to take her idea that far.

"All right," Melissa continued efficiently. "It looks like we've got our theme. The next big question on the agenda is where should we hold the ball? Any ideas? And, no"—she glared at the Beasts—"the graveyard is *not* an option!"

Olivia felt a nudge under the table, and looked over to find Sophia looking at her intently.

"Anyone?" asked Melissa.

Sophia was now pursing her lips and glaring at Olivia, clearly trying to say something with her eyes, but Olivia had no idea what it was.

Sophia sighed and turned to face the table. "How about Ivy's house?" she suggested. "You know, that mansion on top of Undertaker Hill? It has a massive ballroom on the third floor. You can see all Franklin Grove from up there."

Olivia kicked Sophia under the table. "I'm not sure that's a good idea!" she put in hurriedly. "I don't think my parents . . . I mean, parent . . . I mean, dad . . ." She shook her head wildly. Everybody was looking at her. "Well, he won't like it," she finished lamely.

"Who are you kidding, Ivy?" said the girl with the shock of white in her hair. "Your father loves this kind of thing. My parents still talk about the Dead of Winter fund-raiser he planned a few years back."

The girl with the studded collar nodded. "I'll bet he'd even be willing to help out with decorations," she added. "After all, he is one of the top interior designers."

"He redid my aunt's place last year," put in the bald-headed boy. "It looks killer."

Well, Olivia thought, *at least that explains the inside of Ivy's house.* "But a ball for the whole school is a lot of people," she pointed out.

"Don't be so dramatic, Ivy," the girl with the studded collar said. "It's not the *whole school.* It's just the kids in our community from middle and high school. A hundred people, tops."

Olivia suddenly understood why she hadn't seen any posters at school: this was an exclusive all-Goth affair. *How intense!* she thought excit-edly. *Maybe that's why they're being so secretive.*

"Since you came up with the theme and it's your house, Ivy, I think it's only fair that you be head of decorations," Melissa said.

"I still have to ask my dad," Olivia muttered, while thinking, *Head of decorations! How cool is that?*

"All in favor, say aye," Melissa commanded.

Everyone said, "Aye," even the Beasts.

"Great!" shouted Olivia. Wait, her sister wouldn't be so excited. She rolled her eyes. "I mean, *great*," she said sarcastically.

Olivia was still walking on air when she and Sophia emerged from the FoodMart after the meeting. Halfway across the parking lot, Sophia spun around to face her.

"That wasn't like you," she said in a quiet, firm voice.

Olivia's heart sank. *Sophia's seen through the switch!* she thought.

"That idea," Sophia went on slowly. "The way you spoke up. Really, the fact that you came at all." Her lips curled into a smile. "Thank you so much, Ivy!" She started talking really fast. "It is such a seriously big deal to be on the planning committee for the All Hallows' Ball at all, and my best friend"—she grabbed Olivia's hand proudly—"my *best friend*, came up with the theme, is hosting it at her house, and is going to be head of decorations! And guess who she is going to appoint head of photography? This is deadly!" Sophia concluded, throwing her arms around Olivia in a huge hug.

Olivia couldn't help smiling and leaping around with her, at least a little bit.

"Enough!" Sophia cried, throwing her scarf over her shoulder. "I *must* go home and study algebra. But I will talk to you later." She gave a little wave and took off in the dimming autumn light.

Olivia knew she should hurry home, too. She'd promised to be home by seven; her father was grilling veggies on the new barbecue for dinner. But she decided it was okay if she paused for just a second. After all, she had made it through the meeting. Not only that, but she had really *contributed*. Her parents would be proud of her if they knew. She felt like she was really going to love Franklin Grove. That is, as long as Ivy didn't kill her.

As she stopped off in a restaurant's bathroom to change clothes, Olivia prayed that her sister had had a good date with Brendan. Actually, she hoped Ivy was more overjoyed than she'd ever been in her entire life, because, if not, she probably wasn't going to handle Olivia's news very well. After all, not only was Ivy—the official Antiperky—going to have to *plan* the All Hallows' Ball, she had to convince her father to *host* it, too!

CHAPTER 7

Ivy kicked off her boots, fell back on her bed, and grabbed one of her black cat pillows to her chest.

As her head swam, her heart went under.

What did he mean when he said he was scared to death? she wondered.

I can't believe I spilled my drink! But at least I didn't have to answer his question about whether I have a sister.

Was it an accident when his hand brushed against mine on the escalator?

He said we'd keep a running tally in air hockey. Does that mean he's going to ask me out again?

I never want to forget the look on his face when he said good-bye.

The phone rang, making Ivy jump. It rang again.

Maybe it's Brendan! She rolled over and picked it up. "Hello?"

"Greetings, Madam Head of Decorations," Sophia declared dramatically.

Ivy had completely forgotten about Olivia and the meeting. She sat up with a jolt. "Hi, Soph. What's up?"

"The deadliest All Hallows' Ball in history, that's what's up," Sophie replied delightedly.

The All Hallows' Ball? Ivy wondered.

"I'm supposed to be studying," Sophia barreled on, "but I just couldn't stop thinking of ideas. Like, what if you could have your picture taken with a cutout of that short old guy who was Grandpa on *The Munsters*?"

"*The Munsters*?" quavered Ivy.

"You know, that old TV show."

"Uh-huh," Ivy admitted. She was starting to feel seriously ill.

"Or I think it would be killer if we had coffins

near the entrance, and you could get your picture taken getting out of one, right next to your date getting out of *his* coffin. Isn't that killer?" Sophia rattled on.

Ivy was dumbfounded. *What did Olivia do?*

"So?" Sophia asked expectantly. "What do you think?"

"Since when does it matter what I think?" Ivy asked, a little testily.

"Uh, since you came up with the theme, got elected head of decorations, and agreed to have the ball at your house," Sophia answered matter-of-factly.

WHAT? Ivy's head pounded. She lay back down on her bed.

"Speaking of which, did you talk to your dad yet?" Sophia asked.

"No, I did not speak to my dad yet!" Ivy answered incredulously.

After a long pause, Sophia said, "Ivy, are you feeling okay?"

"I . . . er, I'm sorry, Soph. I just . . . have a really grave headache. Can I call you back later?"

Ivy managed, and then she hung up, her hands trembling. *I never should have let Olivia go to that meeting!* she thought in a panic.

But then she thought of Brendan. If she hadn't gone through with the switch, she wouldn't have been able to go on the date. In fact, if it weren't for Olivia, she might never have spoken to Brendan at all.

Ivy let out a heavy sigh. She rummaged through her purse for her phone. She'd saved her sister's number on it when Olivia had borrowed it to call home.

"Abbott residence," Olivia answered perkily.

"It's me," Ivy said.

"Ivy! You're home!" Olivia squealed excitedly. "I tried you like fifteen minutes ago! How was it?"

"It was—" Ivy stopped. "It was *perfect*," she said at last. She heard Olivia gasp as if she'd just opened a wonderful present.

"I knew it," Olivia said softly.

Ivy was suddenly dying to tell her sister everything: where she and Brendan had gone, what he'd said, how he'd smelled, and how he had looked at her when they'd said good-bye. Instead she said, "Don't try to change the subject, Olivia. I *specifically* told you to sit in that meeting and not say anything."

"I know," Olivia said sheepishly. "I'm sorry."

"And not only did you not do that but you landed me the one job at which I'm guaranteed to be a disaster!"

"You won't be a disaster," Olivia protested.

"Oh, come on!" Ivy cried. "Ivy Vega, head of decorations? I don't like pressure, I don't like people, and I *don't* like decorating things."

"But you have great taste," her sister countered.

"Olivia, you don't understand. This is the most important event of the whole year for"—she just caught herself in time—"for our community."

"I'll help," offered Olivia.

"Thanks, but I think I've had enough of your help," Ivy said, rubbing her temples. "Besides," she added, "who says my dad will go for it?"

"Sophia," Olivia answered matter-of-factly. "You never told me your dad's an interior designer. Everybody seemed to think it was right up his alley."

Ivy groaned in frustration. It was true: her dad would be utterly delighted. He was always trying to get her to be more involved in the community. "With a name like Ivy," he was always saying, "you should be getting out and about more."

"I'm really sorry, Ivy. I completely understand why you're upset. I never should have signed you up for something like this. But Sophia says it's cool to be involved with the ball," Olivia said.

"It is," Ivy admitted. "But I can't do it, Olivia. I just can't."

"A few hours ago you said you couldn't go on a date with Brendan Daniels," argued Olivia, "and look how that turned out."

Ivy was speechless. She was still trying to come up with a suitable comeback when she heard her dad pick up the phone.

"Pardon me, Ivy," he said politely, "but it is time for dinner."

"I'll be up in a minute, Dad," Ivy answered softly. Her father hung up, and Ivy sighed. She felt so tired. For a moment she said nothing. "Meet me at Meat & Greet tomorrow at noon," she said finally to her sister, "and I'll let you know what my dad said."

"Great!" Olivia exclaimed on the other end of the phone. "So you'll ask him?"

"I'll see you tomorrow," Ivy finished.

Head aching, Ivy hung up and stood to go to dinner. She walked to the bottom of the stairs like a zombie. Then, suddenly, she imagined Brendan standing on the landing above her, wearing a dashing tuxedo and lounging against the banisters as he waited for her. He looked gorgeous, his dark curls framing his high cheekbones and strong jaw as he glanced around, clearly admiring the decorations. His gaze finally came to rest on Ivy, an adoring look in his eyes.

Ivy shook the thought from her mind, but she couldn't shake the smile that had crept onto her face. She skipped up the stairs to talk to her dad.

★ 🐰 ★

"This place does quite a business," Olivia's father said as Olivia climbed out of the car in front of the Meat & Greet Diner.

Apparently, the Meat & Greet was even more popular for weekend brunch than it was for burgers after school. The line was out the door. Olivia waved good-bye to her dad and squeezed inside to see if her sister had already arrived.

Sure enough, Ivy was sitting at her usual table tucked in the back.

Olivia bounded over. "Hey!" she cried.

Ivy responded with a serious-sounding, "Hello, Olivia."

Right away, Olivia's heart sank. She sat down, ready to learn that they wouldn't be having the All Hallows' Ball at Ivy's house after all. "Your dad said no, didn't he?" she said with a sigh.

Ivy shook her head. "He said yes."

"Yes?" Olivia cried.

"Yes," Ivy confirmed, her face breaking into a smile.

"That's awesome!" Olivia declared.

"And everything's going to be fine," Ivy added lightly.

Wait a minute, Olivia thought. *This doesn't sound like Ivy.* She looked at her sister skeptically. "I thought you thought this was a terrible idea."

"I do." Ivy nodded. "But I've figured out how to fix it."

"You're going to burn me at the stake?" Olivia joked.

Ivy grinned. "Close," she said. "Hereafter, you will pretend to be me for all ball planning meetings and decorating activities."

Olivia blinked. "You mean you want to switch again?"

Ivy nodded.

Suddenly the waitress appeared. Ivy ordered a burger, and Olivia asked for a Greek salad with extra tomatoes.

After the waitress was gone, Olivia said, "What happened to 'you'll never make it past my friends'?"

"I'm willing to take that risk," said Ivy. "Apparently, my friends don't know me very well anyway. *Head of decorations?*" She rolled her eyes.

Olivia thought for a moment. She had to admit, being Ivy at yesterday's meeting had been great fun.

Ivy said, "There are only two more meetings, right?"

"Uh-huh, plus the actual decorating before the ball." *This could work*, she thought.

"Then that's the plan," Ivy said decisively. She flashed that fake mean squint of hers. "You better make me look good."

"For sure," Olivia said distractedly. She was already thinking about how she needed to get started on ideas for the next meeting on Friday.

Friday! she thought with a jolt. "I can't do it!" she blurted. "The meetings are on Fridays, and I have cheerleading practice on Fridays!"

"I know," said Ivy, nodding calmly.

"Please, Ivy. I mean, I know I messed up, but if I don't show at the practices I'll never make the squad!"

"I *know*," Ivy repeated.

"I really, really, really, really, *really* want to be a Devils cheerleader," Olivia said. "You—"

"Olivia," Ivy interrupted, "I'm going to go to your cheerleading practices *for* you."

Olivia was shocked. "You're kidding," she said at last.

"I'm dead serious," Ivy replied, and she looked it.

That's a terrible idea! thought Olivia. She shook

her head briskly. "Talking to a jock at lunch and fooling Charlotte is easy compared to cheering, Ivy. Girls train all year for tryouts. I mean, cheering is totally hard."

"Who made the squad in sixth grade?" Ivy demanded.

The waitress set their food down on the table. "Besides," Ivy went on, "it's not as if it would be for the actual tryout. You'll still get to make the squad all on your own."

Olivia hesitated.

Ivy leaned forward, her burger in one hand. "Olivia, you got me into this mess," she said in a low voice. "Now you have to get me out of it."

"But—" Olivia began.

"The only butt," interrupted Ivy, "is going to be yours, in the seat, at those meetings." She took a big bite of her burger.

"But I thought you hated cheerleading," Olivia persisted.

"I do," admitted Ivy with her mouth full. "But I hate party planning more."

Olivia thought about it while she started eating

her salad. It *was* her fault that Ivy was on the planning committee, and she owed it to her sister to make things right. "I'll do it," she said at last, "but only if you'll practice with me every day after school. We're going to train together."

"Absolutely," said Ivy without hesitating.

"I mean it," Olivia said seriously. "You've got to be squad material if you're going to pretend to be me."

"You bet," Ivy agreed.

While Ivy clearly wasn't fazed, Olivia felt like someone was shaking a pom-pom in the pit of her stomach. There was just so much that could go wrong. "Is this what you felt like yesterday after we talked on the phone?" she asked in a small voice.

"Worse," Ivy answered.

Olivia took a deep breath. *Here we go*, she thought. Then she looked up, all business. "Okay," she said. "That means we only have four days next week to get you into shape. I'm starting you on a strict program for the rest of the weekend. Give me a pen."

"You're giving me homework?" Ivy asked

incredulously, pulling a pen out of her bag and handing it over.

"Sort of," Olivia answered, starting to scribble a list on a napkin. "You have four cheerleading movies to rent and watch before Monday."

CHAPTER 8

"I cannot believe you made me watch a movie called *Go Team Go*," Ivy said. She and Olivia were standing in the hallway after first period Monday morning. "It may have been the gravest eighty-two minutes of my life. That Veronica girl was seriously stupid."

"You were supposed to watch the *cheers*, Ivy," Olivia said. She swung her ponytail. "Anyway, where should we practice this afternoon? I've told my parents I have practice every day after school for the next two weeks."

"Since school's not an option," Ivy said, "let's use my backyard. My dad just landed a big project, so he won't be home early again any time soon."

"Great," Olivia said.

Over her sister's shoulder, Ivy spotted Brendan coming down the hall. Instinctively, she edged behind Olivia.

"What are you doing?" Olivia asked.

Ivy hesitated. "Hiding," she whispered.

To Ivy's horror, Olivia turned around to look.

"Oh, my gosh." Olivia spun back around. "You should see the look on Brendan's face!" She gave Ivy's shoulders a squeeze. "I'll leave you two love-bugs alone," she said and hurried away.

"Hi, Ivy," Brendan said, glancing down at his boots.

"Hey," gulped Ivy, her heart beating wildly.

"How—how was your weekend?" he asked.

"Good," Ivy answered, unable to come up with anything more detailed.

He laughed awkwardly and looked away the moment their eyes met. "Thanks again for coming with me to the mall," he said.

"You're welcome," Ivy answered lamely. She knew her answers must sound seriously dim, but she was just too excited to think straight.

Brendan started pulling the cap on and off a pen he was holding. "So, er . . ."

Suddenly Ivy realized that Brendan Daniels was nervous. She could almost hear his heart pounding. It made him even more gorgeous.

He dropped his pen cap by accident, and it clattered to the floor. They both knelt down to pick it up. Ivy's hand brushed against his.

"Sorry," they both said.

Brendan picked up the cap. "So, what I wanted to ask you is . . ." he began, still kneeling awkwardly.

Ivy leaned forward.

"Will you go with me to the All Hallows' Ball?" Brendan finished.

Ivy's heart stopped. She stared at Brendan, the boy she'd been in love with for three years but only talked to for the first time on Friday. Then her heart restarted with a roar. Brendan was watching her intently as her mind flooded with questions. *What am I going to wear? What if I have to dance? What if I look stupid?* She was lucky she was already on the floor, or she might have fallen over.

Finally, Brendan stood up. "It's okay," he said quietly, nodding in resignation. "I understand if you don't want to go. I—I just hope we can still be friends."

Ivy leaped to her feet. "No!" she cried. "I mean, yes!" She shook her head as if it were surrounded by bees. "I mean, I can't dance!"

Brendan's face lit up like a full moon. "Neither can I," he said. Then he cocked his head and asked, "But have you ever tried dancing with someone else who can't dance?"

Ivy shook her head.

"It's not so bad," Brendan told her. "Look." He took Ivy's hands and placed them on his shoulders; then he put his hands gently on her hips.

Ivy felt like she was touching one of those static electricity things at the science museum. Energy coursed through her, and the hair on the back of her neck stood on end.

Neither of them moved.

"What are we doing?" Ivy murmured at last.

Brendan looked deep into her eyes. "We're not dancing," he whispered.

They stood there like that forever, or at least until Ivy heard the bell for second period ring.

"Then what happened?" Olivia asked, bending forward and putting her palms down on the cool grass. She could feel the muscles stretch in the backs of her legs.

Ivy pulled her foot up behind her. "I was late for art," she replied coyly.

Olivia thought maybe Ivy was blushing, but it might have been the sun. Finally she gave up trying to tell. "Well," she said, hopping up and down on the balls of her feet, "I don't know if that's like the most romantic thing I've ever heard . . . or the *weirdest*."

"Shut up!" Ivy cried.

"Not dancing?" Olivia giggled. Her sister was *so* smitten!

"Stop it!" Ivy said. "It was very . . . sweet."

"I may not have known you long," Olivia said with a grin, "but I already know that 'sweet' is not a word my sister would normally use."

"Sweet," her sister repeated tenderly.

Olivia grabbed Ivy's hand playfully. "Well," she said, "you certainly have reason to . . . CHEER!" She raised both their arms into the air.

Ivy groaned.

Olivia silenced her with a double clap. "Okay, let's get started!" She paced in front of her sister like a drill sergeant. "What's the most important thing to remember when you cheer?"

Ivy thought for a second. "Don't get a wedgie?"

"No," Olivia said. She spoke slowly and carefully, "Never stop smiling!"

"Right." Ivy frowned.

"Let me see it," Olivia commanded.

"Do I have to? Nobody's even watching," Ivy complained.

"Exactly," Olivia said.

Ivy huffed and contorted her mouth into a crooked smile that looked like a four-year-old had dragged a marker across her face. She raised her eyebrows in defiance.

"I bet you don't know the *second* most important thing to remember either." Olivia paused for dramatic effect. "Never, ever touch another cheerleader's . . ."

Her sister's black-lined eyes widened expectantly.

"Poms!"

Ivy's mouth burst into a huge grin.

Olivia shouted, "Hold that smile!" and rushed to show Ivy the first cheer. She'd specifically picked one that she thought her sister would like.

"Ashes to ashes, dust to dust,
Hate to beat you, but we must.
When you're up, you're up.
When you're down, you're down.
When you're messing with the Devils,
You're up (*clap, clap*) side (*clap, clap*) down
(*clap, clap*)!"

Olivia finished with a big smile, her fists raised, her ponytail bobbing. "Okay," she said, "now you try it!"

Her sister skulked into position.

From the neck up, Ivy was even worse than Olivia had feared. She was a total mumbler, and her smile kept sliding off her face.

From the neck down, though, Olivia almost couldn't believe what she saw. Ivy hit every hand-clap in perfect time; her jumps were high; her splits showed great flexibility; and she even threw in a backflip at the end that she stuck perfectly.

Ivy looked at her expectantly.

Olivia put on her best poker face and said, "Let's try another one." This time, she did a much more complicated cheer. The girls on her old squad had called it the Washer-Dryer because it involved so much tumbling. It ended in three consecutive roundoffs.

Ivy did it perfectly on her first try—except that she did four roundoffs. When she finally came to a stop, her back was less than a foot from the wall of her house.

"Wow!" said Olivia.

"Told you so," said Ivy, returning with a smirk on her face and her arms crossed.

"If we can get your yelling and smiling up to speed, we might just get away with this," Olivia admitted.

"Can't I just lip-synch?" Ivy asked, kicking the ground.

Olivia wrinkled her nose. "Sorry, but no."

★ 🐰 ★

By the end of the hour, Olivia had taught Ivy four cheers, which was one more than Olivia had planned for. Ivy was a really quick learner. To end the session, Olivia put her hands on her sister's shoulders and said, "Tonight, I want you to bury your head in your pillow and yell your head off. Okay?"

"I'll do my best," Ivy agreed. They hugged good-bye.

Olivia skirted the side of the house and bounded down the long driveway. She'd promised her mom she'd help make dinner to celebrate the unpacking of the final moving box.

She felt so much better. For the last three days, Olivia had been worried sick about how in the world she was going to train Ivy *and* be ready for tryouts herself. But today's practice had changed all that. With a partner as good as Ivy, they'd both be in stellar shape! She skipped into the cul-de-sac at the end of the driveway.

"Hello, Olivia," a familiar voice said coolly.

Charlotte Brown was standing in the next driveway, which led up to a peach-colored bungalow. Olivia had totally forgotten that she and Ivy were next-door neighbors.

"Hi, Charlotte," Olivia said tentatively.

"Did you have fun at Ivy's house?" Charlotte asked.

Good thing we didn't practice in the front *yard,* Olivia thought. "Yeah. It was great," she said vaguely.

Charlotte shook her head. "I don't get you, Olivia," she said. "You're a good cheerleader. You could really have a future with us. But"—she shrugged—"if you want to be a gravedigger, that's your choice." She turned and started trotting away up the driveway. "Just don't expect any of us normal girls to be in your cult!" she called over her shoulder.

As she headed home, Olivia marveled at how much had changed since she'd first met Charlotte last week. *I can't believe I actually thought Charlotte Brown would be my new best friend,* she thought. *Gross!*

CHAPTER 9

"What about a big box of props for the photographs, so that people can pretend to stake each other?" Sophia asked eagerly as she added a chocolate brownie to her lunch tray.

Ivy tried to nod enthusiastically, but her best friend was driving her seriously batty. Lately the ball was all that Sophia wanted to talk about. Ivy scanned the cafeteria for a place to sit. Holly and Collette were both studying for a test in the library, so Ivy knew she had to do something to avoid an entire lunch debating streamers versus balloons.

She spotted Olivia sitting in the corner with

Camilla Edmunson, who Ivy and Sophia both knew because she occasionally wrote for the school paper. "Let's sit over there," Ivy suggested. At least with them Sophia would have to take a break from the ball.

"With the bunnies?" Sophia said skeptically.

"Why not?" Ivy answered. "You always like Camilla's book reviews."

Sophia shrugged, and they made their way over.

"Hey," said Ivy, with an innocent nod toward Olivia. "Can we sit here?"

"Sure," Camilla replied.

"Totally," Olivia agreed.

As they sat down, Camilla said, "Your last photo essay in the paper was really great, Sophia."

"Thanks," Sophia replied appreciatively. "Speaking of the paper, I read that book you reviewed last week. You know, the one you gave four devils out of five, *The Vortex Effect*? You were right. It sucks."

"Doesn't it?" gushed Camilla.

"Where's your food?" Olivia asked Ivy, gesturing at Ivy's half-empty tray.

"They ran out of burgers," Ivy explained, rolling her eyes. "What kind of school cafeteria runs out of burgers?"

"We should riot," joked Sophia, and everyone laughed.

"Want some of my beef lasagna?" Camilla offered. "My mom made it. It's the best."

Ivy peered into Camilla's Tupperware. It did look really good, and she was dying for something with meat in it. "Okay," she said gratefully. "If you think you have enough."

Camilla slid a generous piece of lasagna onto a napkin and passed it to Ivy.

"Thanks," Ivy said. She scooped up a hunk with her fork and popped it in her mouth. Right away, her tongue felt like it was on fire. She gagged and swallowed to stop the pain.

Oh, no! thought Ivy in a blind panic. *That was the gravest thing I could possibly have done!* Her stomach turned, and she felt ice-cold. She started seeing spots—big black and blue blobs at the corners of her vision.

"Ivy?" Olivia said, leaning across the table. "Are you okay?"

She couldn't answer.

"She looks really pale," Camilla said in a far-away voice. "Like, even paler than normal."

Ivy blinked. Her head was killing her.

Sophia grabbed Ivy's hand and turned to Camilla. "Did that have garlic in it?" she asked urgently.

"I, er, don't know," Camilla stammered. "Maybe."

Sophia stood up. "We have to go."

Ivy felt her friend pull her to her feet. The last thing she heard as Sophia dragged her out of the cafeteria was Olivia's voice calling, "Is she okay?" from a million miles away.

"Do you think she's okay?" Olivia repeated as Ivy and Sophia disappeared out the cafeteria doors.

"I don't know what happened," Camilla said, shaking her head guiltily. "Maybe Ivy's allergic to garlic."

"She looked so ill!" Olivia remarked.

"Everybody says my mom's lasagna's great," Camilla tried to explain. "At least Sophia seemed to know what to do," she added.

"Yeah." Olivia wrung her hands. "I just hope Ivy's *all right*."

After lunch and through the rest of the day, Olivia watched for her sister in the hallways, but she was nowhere to be found. She didn't see Sophia anywhere either.

Olivia started to really worry when Ivy didn't show up for last period. She remembered how, at her old school, somebody's little brother had almost died after accidentally eating a peanut. All through science, Olivia had to fight the urge to rush out of class. She kept staring at the door.

"Olivia?" Mr. Strain was pointing at her with a piece of chalk. "The process by which plants turn sunlight into energy?"

"Er . . . chlorophyll?" Olivia suggested. The entire class chuckled.

It was the longest science class of her life. When the bell finally rang, Olivia had already packed up her things and punched Ivy's phone number into her new cell phone.

She was the first one out the door, hitting Send the moment she crossed the threshold. It rang once. Twice. Three times. *Four times.*

"Hello?" Ivy's sickly voice answered.

"Ivy!" Olivia cried. "Are you okay?"

"Hi, Olivia," her sister said weakly. "I'm all right. I just had a . . . grave reaction to . . . the garlic in Camilla's . . . lasagna."

"You sound *awful*," Olivia told her, leaning against a locker.

"I'll be better . . . in a day or two," Ivy said drily.

Olivia felt tears spring to her eyes. "I was really worried." She gulped.

"Really, I'm okay," Ivy said reassuringly. "I just can't . . . practice today. I'm sorry."

"Don't worry about that," said Olivia. She'd been so worried she'd actually totally forgotten they were supposed to cheer together this afternoon. "Just get better! Do you need anything?"

"No thanks," Ivy whispered. "Just rest."

"I'll call you later," Olivia said.

After she'd hung up, Olivia spotted Camilla by her locker and went over to give her the update. "Ivy's okay," Olivia said. "She went home."

"What happened?" Camilla asked, her eyes wide with concern.

"She's allergic to garlic," Olivia explained. "She needs some time to recover, but she says it's really no biggie."

"I'm so relieved she's all right," Camilla said, sliding a book into her bag. Then she looked up at Olivia. "Are you doing anything after school today?"

"I did have plans," Olivia replied, "but they got canceled."

"Want to go to a book signing at the mall?" Camilla asked, swinging her bag over her shoulder. "It's this guy who's, like, a minor deity in the sci-fi world."

Olivia thought about it for about half a second. Her parents weren't expecting her home until dinner. "Sure." She grinned. "I'd love to."

* 🦇 *

Thursday afternoon, Ivy stretched in her backyard and waited for Olivia to arrive. While she still felt a little stiff from the lasagna incident, she was seriously ready to reenter the land of the living after two days in bed.

She sat down and leaned over her outstretched legs to touch her toes. It had rained the night before, and the still-damp grass soaked through her black sweats, so she scrambled to her feet again.

As she did so, her sister bounded around the corner of the house with an excited, "Hello!"

Ivy smiled, and they hugged tightly.

"You have one bite of garlic and you're out of commission?" Olivia poked her in playful disbelief. "That's insane!"

Ivy stepped back and shrugged uncomfortably. "I had too much garlic as a baby," she mumbled. "It doesn't agree with me."

"That's weird," Olivia said. "Especially because we had the same parents until we were one. And I *love* garlic."

Can she tell I'm lying? Ivy wondered.

Fortunately, her sister didn't say anything more about it. Instead, Olivia did a double clap and said, "Okay, on Monday, you made it pretty clear you can cheer. But your shouting looked more like pouting!"

"Are you rhyming on purpose?" Ivy asked.

"Yes," Olivia replied enthusiastically. "So let's see whether today you can sell the yell!"

Ivy rolled her eyes. Then she stood up straight, turned up the corners of her mouth, and launched into the "Ashes to Ashes" cheer. During the past two days in bed, she'd come up with a trick to help her smile: she imagined the four Beasts standing in a graveyard, wearing nothing but pink briefs that said I'M WITH STUPID on them. It worked like a charm.

"Go, Ivy!" Olivia cheered as Ivy finished. "That was much better! You even smiled!"

"Thanks," Ivy responded, slightly embarrassed.

Olivia patted her on the back and said, "Want to work on roundoff combinations for a new cheer?"

"Okay," said Ivy. They moved closer to the house and turned to face a distant line of thornbushes. Olivia counted down, and together they took a few running steps and leaped into the air.

One, two, three roundoffs. Out of the corner of her eye, Ivy saw Olivia stick her last move.

Deciding to go one better, Ivy put her hand to the ground, ready to push off into a double handspring. But her palm slipped on the rain-slick grass, her arm went out from under her, and suddenly she was flying wildly through the air.

The thornbushes came spinning toward her like a kaleidoscope. "Owww!" Ivy cried as she slammed into them.

Olivia came running. "Ivy!"

"I'm okay," Ivy called, feeling like an utter loser. She stood up from the bushes and brushed herself off. "That's what I get for trying to show off."

"You're hurt!" Olivia exclaimed.

Ivy looked down and saw that her left arm was covered in blood; two deep crimson cuts ran its length. She had been careless. Usually, she would have checked to make sure there weren't any obvious injuries before emerging from the thornbushes, but it was too late now. Instinctively, she put her other hand over the scratches so her sister wouldn't see.

But before she knew it, Olivia was at her side, trying to move her hand away.

"Let me look," Olivia said reassuringly. "I took first aid for my babysitting course last summer."

Olivia pried Ivy's fingers away and gingerly

dabbed at the area with a little towel she had pulled from her waistband.

The blood came away on Olivia's towel, but—just as Ivy knew they would be—the scratches were gone!

"You were bleeding," Olivia said, twisting Ivy's arm around in her hands, looking for a cut. "You were bleeding," she said again in confusion.

Ivy stared at the ground, frantically wondering what she could say.

Olivia shook her head, frowning. "Does it hurt?" she asked.

"No, it's fine. I, er . . ." Ivy stammered. How was she going to explain this?

"You're not cut somewhere else, are you?" Olivia asked, bending to inspect Ivy's legs. "This is so weird," she muttered, clutching the bloody towel in her hands.

Ivy could feel her sister trying to catch her eye now.

"Ivy?" Olivia said, her voice brimming with confusion. "What just happened? Did you . . . did you *heal*?"

I should tell Olivia the truth, Ivy thought. *I don't want to lie to her. She's my twin sister.*

"Ivy, say something!" Olivia demanded in exasperation.

I have to tell her, Ivy decided. "Olivia," Ivy said slowly, meeting her sister's gaze, "I have to tell you a secret."

"*Okay,*" Olivia answered cautiously.

"It's serious," Ivy told her, taking her hand. "I need you to promise you won't tell anyone."

Olivia's eyes searched Ivy's face. "What is it?"

"It's the most important secret you'll ever know," Ivy said simply.

Olivia took a deep breath. "I swear on our sisterhood," she said at last.

Ivy pulled Olivia into the shade of the thornbushes. Then she slowly lifted her hands up to her face and carefully popped out her contact lenses, one after the other.

Olivia put her hand to her mouth. "Your eyes are purple!"

"They're violet," corrected Ivy. She tried to smile. "Olivia," she said, "I'm a vampire."

Olivia put her hands on her hips. "You are not."

Ivy nodded solemnly in response.

"You're a vampire?" Olivia asked, bewildered. "For real?"

"And Sophia's a vampire," Ivy went on. "And the other people in my . . . community: they're vampires, too. We have to wear contact lenses to protect our eyes from the sun."

"Yeah, right," Olivia said. "Like I'm going to believe that vampires have purple eyes!"

"Most don't," Ivy admitted matter-of-factly, putting her contacts back in. "My eyes are special. Bright yellow, luminous green—those are more normal."

"Normal?" Olivia said dumbly.

"Uh-huh," Ivy confirmed.

"That's not in the Count Vira books," Olivia said with a doubtful shake of her ponytail.

"Count Vira is fiction," Ivy replied. "I'm a fact. We all have to wear special sunscreen, too," she went on. "Vampire skin is very pale and sensitive. It's completely different from yours."

"Is that why your arm stopped bleeding?" Olivia asked.

"We heal super quickly," Ivy explained.

Olivia suddenly took a step back. "You're not going to suck my blood, are you?"

Ivy rolled her eyes. "Olivia, I'm your twin sister," she said. "Do you think I'd be practicing *cheerleading* with you if I wanted to suck your blood?"

Olivia came back and examined Ivy's arm closely. "But isn't that what vampires do? Suck blood and kill people?"

"We don't kill people at all. *Ever*," Ivy said seriously. "It's evil! And, besides, the risk of exposing our kind is too great. We haven't sucked blood since the seventeenth century, when they burned half of us at the stake."

"So how do you satisfy your insatiable thirst for hemoglobin?" Olivia pressed.

"*My insatiable thirst for hemoglobin!?*" Ivy repeated incredulously. "You have to start reading better books, Olivia. I go to BloodMart like everyone else. There's one in the basement of FoodMart."

Olivia nodded thoughtfully. Then her eyes lit up. "You have a reflection. You *can't* be a vampire!" she declared triumphantly.

Ivy raised her eyebrows. "That's a myth."

"Oh," said Olivia, deflated. "Do you sleep in a coffin?"

"Yes." Ivy almost blushed. "That myth happens to be true."

"But I saw your bed," Olivia said.

"The quilts and pillows and stuff make it more comfortable when I'm doing homework. There's a coffin underneath," Ivy explained. "When I was little I was utterly jealous of Sophia and her sister's bunk bed coffins," she added wistfully.

"And you getting sick from Camilla's lasagna?" Olivia prompted.

"Was a bit more than an allergic reaction," Ivy admitted.

"You're really serious," Olivia breathed in amazement.

"Completely," Ivy confirmed.

For a moment, Olivia said nothing. Then she gave a queasy smile. "I am *so* glad I didn't have any cherry punch at the ball meeting."

Ivy couldn't help laughing. "Pretty killer secret, huh?" she said.

"Totally," Olivia croaked.

Ivy touched her sister's arm. "Olivia, by telling you this, I've broken the First Law of the Night. A vampire is *never* supposed to reveal her true self to an outsider. I could get into serious trouble if anybody ever finds out that I have"—Ivy paused—"and you could, too."

Olivia nodded bravely. "I won't tell," she said. Then a weird look crossed her face.

"Are you freaked out?" Ivy asked.

"If we're twins," Olivia said slowly, "does that mean that *I'm* a vampire?"

Ivy had been asking herself that question for a week. She shook her head. "There's no way, Olivia. You love garlic; you have normal skin; you have regular blue eyes; and, on top of it all, you're a vegetarian! You're the least vampy person on earth."

"But you're still sure we're twins, right?" Olivia asked.

"Absolutely," Ivy said. "I won't pretend to understand it, but I know I'm a vampire and you're a bunny. We just happen to also be identical twins."

"So that's what a bunny is," Olivia murmured distractedly.

This is a lot for Olivia to take in all at once, Ivy realized. "Maybe now that you know," she said, "swapping places isn't such a good idea. Maybe you shouldn't go to any more ball meetings. I'll do it. You focus on cheering."

Olivia shook her head. "No," she said firmly, "I can do it. I promised you." Suddenly, her eyes rested on Ivy's mouth. Olivia bent her head down a little, and Ivy thought for a second that her sister was trying to look up her nose. Then Ivy realized that wasn't what Olivia was doing at all.

"Are you looking for fangs?" Ivy demanded.

Olivia smiled sheepishly. "Maybe."

Ivy rolled her eyes. "We get our incisors filed down. And just so you know," she added, "my face never gets gross and bumpy like the 'vampires' on *Buffy*."

Olivia nodded thoughtfully.

She needs time to get used to this, Ivy thought. "I think we're done cheering for today," she said aloud.

"But we only just started," Olivia protested halfheartedly.

"It's okay," Ivy said. "Really. I'm ready for

tomorrow. I have the moves. I can shout. I can even smile. You said it yourself."

Olivia's eyes flickered uncertainly.

"Are you sure you still want to go through with it?" Ivy asked.

Her sister grinned. "Are you worried I'll freak out in front of all your friends?"

"A little," Ivy admitted.

Olivia looked her in the eye. "Trust me," she said. "I can handle it." They hugged. "After all, you know what they say," Olivia continued. "Blood is thicker than water."

Ivy couldn't resist. "And better tasting, too!"

CHAPTER 10

In math the next morning, Mr. Langel stood in front of the board, telling the class how to calculate a rectangle's area. He started doing an impression of the Count from *Sesame Street*. "One! Ha-ha-ha!" he declared, smiling.

But Olivia couldn't roll her eyes as she usually did at Mr. Langel's sense of humor. *Could he be a vampire?* she wondered, looking at him suspiciously. After all, his hairline descended into what her mom called a widow's peak—a point in the center of his forehead—which made him look vaguely vampiric. Olivia wondered what color his eyes really were. She pictured him climbing out of a coffin earlier that morning, pajamas still on.

Then she realized that if her goofy math teacher could be a vampire, anyone could! She turned her attention to a stocky Goth boy with an earring and spiky hair sitting at a nearby desk. His hand rested next to his notebook, and there was a leering skull-and-crossbones ring on his pinky. Now that she thought about it, Olivia realized that she'd never seen him open his mouth. Was it because he hadn't had his fangs filed?

She could deal with her sister being a vampire, because she knew Ivy would never do anything to hurt her. It was all the other vampires at Franklin Grove Middle School that Olivia was suddenly worried about. She surreptitiously counted the number of other students in the class: twenty-one possible vampires. She pulled her cardigan more tightly around herself.

What about the cheerleaders? she wondered. Nobody said a vampire couldn't wear pink. Besides, if anyone had some evil in her, it was Charlotte Brown. *Now I'm being ridiculous*, Olivia told herself. *No way is Charlotte cool enough to be a vampire!*

She looked down at her blank paper and wrote, "VAMPIRES DO NOT EAT BUNNIES" ten times without stopping. It sort of helped, except that, when she was done, she realized she'd missed out on how to calculate the area of a trapezoid.

By the end of class, Olivia was obsessing about the ball planning meeting after school. Everyone was nice to Ivy, but what if they discovered she was an impostor? What if they found out that she knew their secret? Ivy had said there could be trouble. . . .

Quickly Olivia tried to think of some sort of protection she could take with her, just in case. She had a nearly empty nail polish bottle in her purse. She thought maybe she could empty it and then fill it with holy water. But, then, what if that was a myth, too? And where was she going to get holy water, anyway? *Would a pencil count as a stake?* she asked herself. She did have two of those in her purse. *Garlic!* she thought suddenly. At least she knew *that* wasn't a myth.

At lunch, Olivia was hoping for a garlic-infused daily special, but no luck. The specials board announced that today it was crab salad, and as Olivia read it something clicked inside her head. *I get it!* she thought. *Vampires are just different kinds of humans, just like crabs and lobsters are different kinds of crustaceans! They're pretty much the same thing: one big happy crustacean family!* And from then on, Olivia felt much better.

She smiled at everybody she saw for the rest of the afternoon, right up to when she grinned goofily at Ivy at the beginning of science.

"How are you?" Ivy asked in a low voice.

"Great!" Olivia said brightly. "It's like you're a lobster!"

Ivy clearly didn't get it, but she didn't press. "Are you still up for the planning meeting this afternoon?" she whispered.

"For sure," Olivia said. "I can totally handle the vamp—" Ivy's eyes widened. Olivia coughed and lowered her voice. "The meeting," she said instead.

At the end of class, Olivia followed her sister into the girls' bathroom.

After they'd switched clothes, Ivy stood looking in the mirror. "Now I wish I *didn't* have a reflection," she said, pulling Olivia's pink gym shirt away from her chest. Then she leaned forward with an eyeliner pencil to do Olivia's eyes. "Remember what you said about cherry punch at the meeting?"

"Uh-huh?" Olivia said.

"Myth," Ivy said simply. "Vampires don't just eat meat and drink blood. You can eat the crackers or chips or whatever's there."

"Okay," said Olivia, feeling just a little less nervous.

"Is there anything else you need to know?" Ivy asked.

Questions raced to the front of Olivia's mind and raised their hands eagerly. Finally, she picked one. "Are all Goths vampires?"

"In Franklin Grove? Not all but most," Ivy told her.

"What about everybody else?"

"Bunnies, like you," Ivy answered matter-of-factly.

"Are you immortal?" Olivia asked.

"That's a tough one." Ivy put Olivia's bag down. "Not really. But I might get to see the day people live on Mars."

"What can kill you?" Olivia wanted to know.

"What can kill *you*?" Ivy countered. "Listen, Olivia, vampires are people, too."

Olivia nodded. "I know. Like you're a lobster and I'm a crab," she said automatically. "But we're both crustaceans."

"*No*," Ivy said. "I didn't say we were *seafood*. I said we were *people*. With hearts and souls and everything. We're into life, liberty, and the pursuit of happiness just like everyone else. We don't even talk about it among ourselves that much. It's like you being a vegetarian. That's not such an enormous deal, right?"

"Right," Olivia admitted. *Totally. No biggie.* "Thanks, Ivy." Olivia scrunched up her nose. "I guess this vampire thing does take some getting used to."

Ivy assumed a vacant look. *"Really?"* she squealed in her cheerleader voice.

⋆ 🐇 ⋆

Even though she knew she had nothing to fear, the hair on the back of Olivia's neck stood on end the moment she and Sophia came in sight of the towering FoodMart sign. Sophia was talking excitedly about the ball as they walked, but Ivy's words were the only ones Olivia could hear: "I go to BloodMart like everyone else. There's one in the basement of FoodMart."

Olivia imagined a huge, dim underground crypt, filled with enormous vats of swirling red liquid. Spigots dripped gruesomely, and blood-soaked napkins littered the floor. Before she knew it, she and Sophia were walking through the store doors and it was too late to flee.

As they walked down aisle nine, questions flooded Olivia's mind. How much blood would be needed to satisfy every vampire in Franklin Grove? How many vampires were there in Franklin Grove, anyway? Dozens? Hundreds? *Thousands?*

She and Sophia came upon the same nose-ringed stock boy with the midnight stubble.

Maybe that wasn't cranberry juice he was stacking after all! Olivia thought. Her heart raced. *He must be a vampire since he opens the door. What if he can smell my fear?* She put her hand to her neck and started hyperventilating.

Sophia gave her a weird look. "You're breathing like a horse," she said. Then she turned to the stock boy and said, "Pumpernickel." He obediently unlocked the staff door, and Olivia scurried past him, trying to avoid eye contact.

The dark staircase creaked with every step. Olivia thought she heard laughter, then creatures scurrying in the walls, then the sound of liquid running ominously in pipes. She was scared of tripping and tumbling down the stairs, but she was even more scared of placing a hand on the wall to steady herself. What if it was damp?

At last they reached the narrow hallway at the bottom. Olivia trailed farther and farther behind, terror making Ivy's boots feel even heavier than usual. She passed the first mysterious unmarked door. It was huge and made of dark, brushed metal. It also had a slot to look through so that those inside could see who was outside wanting to come in. The shutter over the slot was closed, but Olivia could hear talking and laughing from a crowd inside.

BloodMart! Olivia thought. *On the other side of that door, vampires are thirstily drinking BLOOD!*

She lurched forward, feeling sick. She put her hands on her knees. Ivy's black fishnet stockings crawled like spiders beneath her fingers.

"Will you come on?" Sophia called from up ahead.

Olivia thought if she tried to stand up again right now she'd puke.

Sophia's footsteps came closer. "Ivy, relax," she said. "I know you have cold feet about being head of decorations, but it's just a meeting. Besides, you're already doing a killer job."

Then she grabbed Olivia's hand and dragged her to the door at the end of the hall.

The vampires were waiting within: Vera, with her startling shock of white hair, Raymond, with his fiendishly bald head, Anise, as gaunt and hollow eyed as an ex-lover of Count Vira. The Beasts, looking more bloodthirsty and beastly than ever.

Melissa, with her officious manner and disarmingly chunky glasses, offered Olivia some punch. Olivia declined. "Oatmeal raisin cookie?" Melissa tried. Olivia shook her head like a zombie.

Now all the vampires were taking their places around the sacrificial slab of a table.

"May the Secret be cloaked in darkness," Melissa intoned solemnly.

"And never see light of day," came the response.

Olivia collapsed into her seat.

"Okay, people," Melissa began, flipping through her notes. "First item on the agenda is decorations. Ivy?"

Olivia couldn't speak. All the vampires were looking at her with their contact-lens-covered eyes.

"Ivy?" Melissa said again.

Sophia pinched her hard, and Olivia jumped. She reached into Ivy's black velvet messenger bag and pulled out her white All Hallows' Ball—Decorations folder.

The papers rustled in Olivia's trembling hand. "Take one and pass them on," she whispered.

Olivia stumbled through her presentation. She'd organized her ideas into two categories: "Big Things," which included stuff like the centerpieces—fake tombstones featuring celebrity vampires' names, surrounded by bouquets of white lilies—and "Little Things," which included random stuff like rubber spiders, bats, cobwebs, flaming torches, and so on.

Even through her haze, Olivia could tell that the committee, in its Goth way, was pleased. Almost against her will, she started feeling better.

Oh, my gosh, she thought nervously, *I might actually make it through this meeting without losing my mind, being bitten by a vampire, or driving a stake through anyone's heart!*

She'd saved the best idea for last: a bunch of old vampire movie posters she'd found on eBay.

"That sucks!" Anise declared, and everyone nodded. Olivia smiled in spite of herself.

One of the Beasts cleared his throat. "I have an idea," he said, a devilish grin spreading across his face.

Olivia's pulse quickened.

He held up a long, pale finger. "A decoration that's cheap and plentiful."

"Let's hear it," Melissa invited reluctantly.

"Something better than posters." The Beast leered at Olivia. "How about we round up a bunch of dead bunnies from the morgue and line the walls with *them*?"

The other Beasts burst into laughter.

Olivia's stomach churned.

Melissa seethed. "You guys are disgusting!"

Raymond balled up his list and chucked it at the boy.

I have to get out of here! Olivia thought. She leaped up from her chair, blurted, "Sorry" to Sophia, and bolted out of the room.

She raced down the narrow hallway, its walls closing in around her. On the stairs, she tripped and skinned her knee, but she just scrambled to her feet and kept running.

She burst out through the doors of FoodMart and finally slowed to a stop. She leaned against the outside of the building, taking deep breaths of fresh air.

A few seconds later, Olivia heard someone coming up behind her. She spun around, ready to fight for her life, but it was just Sophia.

"What's *wrong* with you?" Ivy's friend asked.

Olivia didn't answer. She was breathing too hard.

Sophia shook her head and said, "You've been acting strange all afternoon. It's one thing for Ivy Vega to be out of her element at social functions, but my best friend has *never in her life* fled from a room." She stepped closer and peered into Olivia's eyes.

Olivia looked away.

Sophia said, "What's going on?"

"Nothing!" Olivia gulped.

"What *is* going on?" Sophia repeated more forcefully.

"Everything's totally fine!" Olivia squealed hysterically.

Sophia narrowed her eyes.

I just said "totally," thought Olivia.

"Did you just say 'totally'?" demanded Sophia.

Olivia sank down on the curb. It was obvious that Sophia knew something weird was going on. She was going to have to confess. "I'm not Ivy," she muttered in defeat.

"What?" said Sophia.

"I'm Olivia Abbott."

Sophia grabbed Olivia's arm. "What have you done with my best friend?" she demanded anxiously.

"Nothing!" Olivia snapped, twisting out of her grasp. "She's at cheerleading practice," she admitted.

Sophia was speechless for a moment. Then she sat down beside Olivia on the curb. "I'm listening," she said.

It took a long time to tell the whole story: discovering they were twins, switching identities, Charlotte Brown, Ivy's date with Brendan, the ball. In the middle of it all, Sophia was nice enough to go inside and buy Olivia some aspirin and a Diet Coke.

After getting over her initial shock that Ivy had a twin sister, Sophia seemed to take the news surprisingly well—except that Olivia left the most awkward part for last.

"And then yesterday," Olivia said slowly, "Ivy told me what kind of person she is."

"What do you mean?" Sophia asked innocently.

"What kind of people you *all* are."

Sophia looked thoughtful for a second. "Goths?"

"No, the *really secret* thing," Olivia said meaningfully.

"Oh!" Sophia's eyes opened wide. "She told you *that*?"

"Yup," Olivia said guiltily. "I wasn't supposed to tell anyone. She said we could both get into big trouble."

"She never should have told you," Sophia said firmly.

"She didn't have a choice," Olivia responded. She shut her eyes and let out a heavy sigh. "This is all my fault." She thought she was going to start crying, but then she felt Sophia's hand on her shoulder.

"Don't worry," Sophia said quietly. "I won't tell anyone."

"Really?" Olivia said, opening her eyes.

"Really," Sophia said sincerely. "Ivy's my best friend."

"And you're not mad?" Olivia asked.

"A little," Sophia admitted with a shrug. "Ivy could have told me she'd found her long-lost twin sister. I feel like I've been missing all the fun. But at least this explains why Ivy was suddenly so good at party planning!" She peered at Olivia's face. "You really had me fooled. I mean, I didn't notice any resemblance between you and Ivy at all."

Olivia smiled. "That spray-on pale stuff does wonders."

Sophia laughed and stood up. "Come on," she said.

"Where are we going?" Olivia asked, getting to her feet.

"Cheerleading practice," Sophia replied. "If Ivy's hopping around like a bunny, I need to see it!"

CHAPTER 11

Ivy stuck the final move of another cheer, yelled, "Fight!" and thrust her arms in the air. She could hear Charlotte panting desperately beside her.

The look on Charlotte's pink face when Ms. Barnett put Ivy front and center in the formation—right in the captain's spot—had been truly unforgettable. It was enough to plaster a 150-watt smile on Ivy's face for the rest of practice. She turned it up.

"Good, girls!" shouted Ms. Barnett.

Ivy had been sinking her teeth into every cheer. Olivia would be so proud.

A few cheerleaders' boyfriends clapped from

the stands. Ivy thought, *I wish Brendan were here, too.* Then she remembered, with a pang of regret, that he'd never even know.

"A Little Birdie!" called Ms. Barnett, and the cheerleaders launched into another cheer.

Ivy was raising herself from a split when out of the corner of her eye she saw the gym doors open. In walked Olivia . . . with Sophia.

Questions raced through Ivy's mind. *Did Sophia figure it out? Does anybody else know? Are we going to have to leave town? What about Brendan? Is Sophia mad?*

Ivy suddenly realized she should be spinning around. She was rushing to catch up to the other girls when Charlotte Brown crashed into her, hard.

"What are you *doing?*" Charlotte shrieked as the cheer ground to a halt. "You're supposed to be over there! What is your problem?"

"Charlotte!" yelled Ms. Barnett.

The Energizer Bunny shut her trap.

"If you're going to be on this squad, I expect to see some teamwork!" Ms. Barnett scolded. "You girls will talk to your fellow cheerleaders with respect!"

"Yes, Ms. Barnett," Charlotte said, staring at the floor.

"And next time, Charlotte"—Ms. Barnett tapped her clipboard—"you'll try to be more aware of the other girls."

Charlotte looked like her eyes were going to pop out of her head. "But it was her fault!" she protested, pointing at Ivy.

"I am *not* interested in playing the blame game," Ms. Barnett said coolly. Then she raised her eyebrows and scanned the rest of the squad. "I hope you've all learned something today, and not just about handclaps and tumbling. See you at practice next Friday." She gave a double clap. Dismissed.

Charlotte stalked off with a grim look, leaving Ivy to beeline it to the back of the gym.

Sophia looked angry. "I cannot believe . . ." She stamped her foot.

Ivy's heart sank into her stomach.

". . . that all I got to see was half a cheer!" Sophia concluded, a grin spreading across her face. "At least I got some pictures," she sang.

Ivy shook her head. "You did not."

162

"Oh, yes, I did," her friend replied.

Ivy herded Sophia and Olivia out of the gym and down the hall to the bathroom.

"What happened?" Ivy said the moment they were safely inside.

"I'm sorry, Ivy!" Olivia blurted.

Sophia stepped forward and said, "Olivia's not the one who should be sorry."

Olivia looked from Sophia to Ivy and back again, then disappeared into a stall to change.

Sophia's teasing smirk was gone. "You're the one who should be sorry," she told Ivy. She shook her head, and her bottom lip started to quiver. "Why didn't you tell me about Olivia?"

"I didn't know how," Ivy whispered.

"I'm your *best friend*," said Sophia, her eyes filling with tears. "Did you think I'd be jealous?"

"No," Ivy said, her voice catching in her throat. "I was just waiting for the right time. And then"—her voice trembled—"once I'd told Olivia everything, I didn't think I'd ever be able to tell anyone about her. Even you."

Sophia rolled her eyes. "You're not the only vamp in history to break the First Law, Ivy."

"But I bet I'm the only one in Franklin Grove," Ivy said sorrowfully.

Sophia sighed and wiped her cheek. She shook her head. "No, you're not." With a deep breath, she continued, "I told that bunny boy I thought I was in love with two summers ago."

"Billy Coddins?"

Sophia nodded. "He didn't believe me. I think he thought I was crazy. I got dumped the next day." She grinned tearily.

Ivy was stunned. "You never told me that!"

Sophia grabbed a paper towel and blew her nose. "I guess you and I both had secrets."

Ivy hugged Sophia tightly. "Best friend," she whispered in her ear.

"Best friend," Sophia whispered back.

"Sorry, you two," Olivia's voice interrupted timidly. "But I'm freezing in here!" Her hand was sticking out from under the stall door with Ivy's clothes.

Ivy and Sophia both burst into laughter.

After Ivy and Olivia were back to their usual selves, Sophia said, "Well, seeing Ivy smile and bounce like a bunny was pretty much the highlight of middle school for me—even better than sixth grade. Thanks for making it all possible, Olivia."

Olivia grinned. "You're welcome." She laughed.

Sophia turned to Ivy. "How about we give our honorary Goth here a proper tour of Franklin Grove?"

"Killer idea," Ivy agreed.

★ 🐰 ★

As the three of them strolled through the center of town, Ivy ticked off all the stores that were vampire friendly for her sister. "Gool's Autobody, Shredders Convenience, Red Mark Cleaners—"

"Don't forget the Juice Bar," Sophia interrupted.

"They really mean it when they say 'blood' oranges," Ivy acknowledged. "Tranzil Pharmacy . . ." she continued.

"Wait," said Olivia. "That can't be one. It's where my mom goes."

"It's not all black-and-white, Olivia," Sophia told her. "Lots of stores serve bunny customers up front, and then have a vampire place in the back. Our community is fully integrated—it has been for more than a hundred years. We're your doctors, your lawyers . . ."

"Your movie stars," Ivy put in.

"Who?" Olivia cried. "Which movie stars?"

Sophia turned abruptly. "We could tell you, but then we'd have to bite you," she said with a mischievous grin.

Olivia skipped over a crack in the sidewalk. "So what can vampires do that other people can't?" she asked.

"Ah, let us count the ways," Ivy said dramatically. "Superhuman strength."

"Superior agility," Sophia said in a high British accent.

"A keen sense of hearing," Ivy added.

Sophia flourished her arms. "Classical beauty." Ivy and her friend both batted their eyelids.

Then Ivy gestured across the main square. "See that guy sitting on the steps of the post office?"

"Uh-huh." Olivia nodded.

"He's been sitting there for nearly one hundred fifty years."

"You're not serious!" cried Olivia.

"You're right, she's not, but he is really old."
Sophia chuckled.

Ivy was surprised by how much fun it was to initiate her sister into the vampire world. She'd never had a chance to explain all these things before.

"So," Olivia asked, "what's the deal with the aging thing? Do you live forever or not?"

Sophia looked at Ivy. "You answer. You're younger."

"Only by four months," Ivy protested. She turned to Olivia. "Remember how those scratches on my arm healed last week? That's the key. We call it RSH, rapid self-healing."

Olivia nodded.

Ivy went on. "We grow at the same rate as humans until we reach adulthood—"

"College." Sophia winked.

"—and then we start aging very slowly."

"My dad's two hundred twelve years old," Sophia said, swinging jauntily around a lamppost.

Olivia looked impressed. "Can you die?" she asked.

"RSH obliterates most injuries," Ivy explained.

"But if the healing process is thwarted—say, because someone leaves you out in the sun for hours, chained to a rock, without any sunscreen, or somebody cuts off your head and moves it to a different town from your body—"

"Ew!" said Sophia.

"That's pretty fatal," Ivy concluded.

"Cool!" Olivia said.

"Depends which town your head's in," Sophia joked.

"So how do I become one?" Olivia asked.

Ivy couldn't tell if her sister was serious, and she paused for a moment before answering. "It's not easy," she said at last, a tinge of genuine disappointment fluttering inside her. Ever since she'd met Olivia, she'd been trying not to think about the fact that one day, her sister would no longer be with her.

"You have to be born one," Sophia explained. "That's what makes you two a complete mystery."

"But what if a human gets bitten?" Olivia asked.

"Doesn't happen," Ivy said, "at least, not anymore."

"Very last century," Sophia chimed in.

"But if it did?" Olivia pressed.

"They'd probably die," Ivy admitted. "But if not," she went on, "they'd become one of us."

★ ◆ ★

The FoodMart sign appeared in the distance, and Olivia smiled to herself. She was on her way to meet Sophia in the parking lot for the last ball planning meeting, and, over her shoulder, a black faux-leather duffel bag was filled near to bursting with supercool decorations to show the committee.

Olivia couldn't get over how quickly the past week had whizzed by. Between meeting Ivy in the afternoons to practice cheering, trying to stay on top of her schoolwork, and her work for the planning committee, Olivia hadn't had a moment's rest.

She'd told her parents that she was head of decorations for a school dance, which was at least partly true. Her mom got excited about buying a dress until Olivia hastily explained that it was exclusively for older students, and she wouldn't be attending.

Every evening, Olivia's mother, who'd been prom queen in high school, spent hours online with Olivia, finding and ordering ball decorations being sure to stick to the ball's budget. Then, when Olivia finally got to bed, she couldn't fall asleep right away because she was busy thinking about the whole new world of vampires she had discovered. Count Vira totally paled in comparison.

Sophia was waiting in front of the FoodMart doors. Olivia linked arms with her, and together they went inside. As they made their way down aisle nine, Olivia asked if she could be the one to say "pumpernickel" today.

"No way," said Sophia with a serious look. "If an outsider says the password, they burst into flames!"

Olivia gasped.

"Just kidding," Sophia said, laughing. "Go for it."

At the meeting, everybody loved the decorations, especially the bats, which were totally lifelike and only cost thirty cents apiece.

"Where did you *get* these?" Vera asked in a dumbstruck voice, turning one over in her pale hand. "It's so real."

"At a website that supplies museums and zoos," Olivia answered. "Liquidation sale."

At one point, the Beasts tried to butt in with another of their grisly ideas, but Olivia stopped them cold with one of Ivy's death squints. They didn't say another word.

When she finished showing what she'd brought, the committee burst into applause. Olivia didn't even know that Goths *could* spontaneously clap with enthusiasm. She was thrilled.

"Great work, Ivy," Melissa said. "I can't wait for next Friday night."

Sophia nudged Olivia's leg approvingly under the table.

After the meeting ended, Olivia and Sophia made a quick exit. Olivia ducked behind the FoodMart and changed into her normal clothes, while Sophia stood guard; Olivia only had fifteen minutes to get to the mall for a shopping date with Camilla.

She stuffed Ivy's outfit in the duffel with all the decorations and handed it to Sophia, who said, "You're getting pretty good at this."

"Aren't I?" said Olivia.

A half hour later, Olivia was standing in the bookstore with Camilla when her cell phone rang.

"Hey, Ivy!" Olivia said brightly, answering the phone and stepping into the crowded mall corridor to talk. "What's up? How was practice?"

"Terrible!" Ivy's voice crackled.

Olivia stiffened. "What happened?"

"It didn't go anything like last week!" Ivy sounded totally distraught. "I was running late," she said, "and by the time I finished making myself pink, I couldn't find your pom-poms. I looked everywhere, Olivia. Finally, I just had to go to practice without them."

"Oh, no," Olivia winced. *A cheerleader never loses her poms!* she thought.

"I might as well have bitten someone. Ms. Barnett gave me this eternal lecture about commitment and responsibility," Ivy went on.

Olivia shuddered.

"And then it just got worse from there," Ivy said miserably. "I was so flustered I forgot the words to one of the cheers."

Olivia closed her eyes.

"I'm sorry, Olivia." Her sister sounded on the verge of tears. "Ms. Barnett seemed utterly disappointed. It would have been a complete loss if it weren't for Camilla."

"Camilla?" Olivia's eyes snapped open and she spun around to look through the bookstore window. There were her friend's golden curls in the sci-fi section. "I'm at the mall with her right now!" she whispered.

"Oh, I wondered what she meant when she said she'd see me at five," Ivy responded.

"What was she doing at practice?" Olivia asked.

"Maybe she came to watch you," Ivy replied. "Anyway, she'd seen some poms lying in the hallway and ran to get them for me—I mean, you."

"Well, I'd better go and thank her!" Olivia said.

Right at that moment, Camilla smiled and waved at her. Olivia waved back sheepishly.

"At least that puts an end to my cheerleading career. I'm never doing *that* again," Ivy remarked gloomily.

"You sure?" Olivia teased, turning away from the window. "It's not too late for you to try out. You could have your very own poms!"

"No, thank you," Ivy said, sounding horrified.

"I just hope everything goes okay on Saturday." Olivia sighed.

"You're going to make the squad, Olivia," Ivy responded confidently. "I know it. Even with me biting at practice. My bet's on you for captain."

"I don't know about that," Olivia said. "But I'll give it my best—" Olivia broke off because she could not believe her eyes; Charlotte Brown was coming her way in a hideous pink tube top, Allison and Katie in tow!

"Hold on," Olivia murmured into her phone.

Charlotte wheeled up with Katie and Allison on either side. "Too bad about Olivia's poms today," she taunted, as if Olivia weren't standing right in front of her. "Katie, Allison, what is the second most important thing to remember in cheerleading?"

"Never touch another cheerleader's poms!" Katie and Allison chorused.

Charlotte put her hand to her mouth in mock horror. "Oops!" She shrugged. "I guess some rules are made to be broken." The three girls tittered idiotically and were gone.

Olivia narrowed her eyes as she gazed after them. "Ivy," she said into her phone, "I think I know who took my poms."

CHAPTER 12

After school on the day of the All Hallows' Ball, Ivy sat on the stairs underneath the basement window of her room, in her black kimono, waiting for Olivia. She'd hardly slept at all the night before. When she'd been practicing cheering with her sister every day, she had successfully avoided thinking about the ball. But ever since her final performance as a cheerleader, dread had swallowed her whole.

She kept trying to keep the facts straight in her mind. *The All Hallows' Ball is tonight. It is at my house. Brendan Daniels is my date. I am head of decorations.* Every single time, she would forget where she had begun and have to start over.

Finally she gave up. She just couldn't face reality; it was like trying to look at the sun. At least Olivia was sneaking over to do all the decorating.

Suddenly she heard a tap on the glass. Ivy pulled aside the curtain and opened the window.

"Hiya!" said Olivia, thrusting an enormous cardboard box into Ivy's hands.

"What's this?" Ivy asked.

"What do you think?" Olivia answered. "More decorations!"

Olivia climbed inside, dragged in another huge box, and pulled the window shut behind her. They dropped the boxes on the landing, and then Ivy led her sister down the stairs.

"You don't look so good," Olivia said.

"Thanks," Ivy replied sarcastically. "Maybe I'll call in sick."

"You wouldn't dare!" Olivia exclaimed.

"Why did I agree to this?" Ivy muttered. She tossed Olivia a can of Pale Beauty.

Olivia shook the can. "We should really start buying this stuff in bulk," she said thoughtfully.

"As if," Ivy answered glumly. While Olivia sprayed her arms, Ivy said, "My dad's raring to go. This is like the most A-positive thing that's ever happened to him." She tried to sound as resentful as possible.

Olivia pulled on a black tank top. "I know," she said obliviously. "I'm so excited."

Ivy sighed heavily. *I wish I didn't have to go tonight,* she thought.

Olivia looked up, almost like she could hear what Ivy was thinking. "Ivy, in a few hours you're going to a dance with the boy you've always wanted. Can't you see? It's your night to shine!"

"I don't want to shine," Ivy sulked.

"Too late," Olivia said. "You already do."

Ivy shook her head. "But I didn't do any of this."

"And I didn't go to cheerleading practice," Olivia countered. "We're a team, Ivy. We did this *together*. That doesn't make it less good." She grinned. "In fact, it makes it even better."

Ivy nodded and tried to smile.

"The only thing you have to do tonight," Olivia continued, "is have fun. I'll take care of the rest."

Ivy took a deep breath. She knew her sister was

right. *The All Hallows' Ball is tonight. It is at my house. Brendan Daniels is my date. I am head of decorations.*

Ivy blinked. "Want to see my dress?" she asked tentatively.

Olivia smiled. "Obviously!"

* 🐰 *

Olivia stretched and stretched, but she couldn't quite reach the corner of the stone arch to tack up the last cobweb.

"Allow me," Ivy's father called from down below. He marched over to another ladder and slid it into place next to hers.

Olivia had been decorating the upstairs ballroom with Mr. Vega for the last few hours, but she still could not get over him. He looked like he'd walked right out of a classic black-and-white vampire film but the kind that's more love story than monster movie. He resembled a pale Antonio Banderas, and his voice was impossibly smooth.

He wore a tailored dark suit jacket over a flowing white shirt and black jeans. Olivia thought of her own father in his short-sleeved plaid polyester shirts and cringed.

"Thanks," she said as Mr. Vega pinched the corner of the web from her fingers.

He hung it gracefully. Then he spun around and leaned back against the top rung of his ladder. "Shall we admire your work?"

Olivia looked over her shoulder and took in the enormous ballroom below. The classic movie posters on the stone walls were illuminated by tiny spotlights. Round black tables dotted the room, tombstones rising from them evocatively. Bats hung at all levels in the air. In each corner of the room, there was a huge coffin lined with dark purple satin that overflowed its sides luxuriantly—a special last-minute touch of Mr. Vega's. Olivia had filled each one with party favors, like plastic fangs, temporary neckbite tattoos, and extra bats.

Olivia felt like cheering. Everything looked awesome!

"Now that is the sort of smile," Mr. Vega mused, "I have rarely seen on your face."

Olivia tried to stop grinning, but she couldn't.

"So, daughter," he said, "you have said nothing of your date."

"You mean Brendan?" Olivia asked nervously as she climbed down the ladder.

"Ah, Brendan. I wondered when you would reveal his identity," Mr Vega remarked.

Oops, thought Olivia.

"Tell me. What is he like?" Mr. Vega continued.

Olivia didn't know how to answer.

"In a world that is so open to you," he mused, "you need not always keep the contents of your heart closed."

"He's really cu—" Olivia stopped herself. "Handsome," she finished.

"I am sure."

"And . . . romantic," Olivia added.

"Oh?" Mr. Vega's dark eyes sparkled.

Olivia remembered something her sister had said. "The way he asked me to the ball was really . . . sweet."

Ivy's father smiled. "I am glad for you, Ivy."

Olivia suddenly felt weird talking about Brendan this way. He wasn't *her* boyfriend, after all. She glanced at the enormous clock above the ballroom entrance. "I should go get ready," she said.

Mr. Vega nodded. "Yes, of course."

Outside the ballroom, Olivia descended the enormous staircase to the first floor. She was walking past the front doors on her way to the basement when she was stopped in her tracks by the momentary booming of a pipe organ. She was about to continue on her way when the organ music rang out again, the same brief ornate musical phrase as before.

"Ivy?" Mr. Vega called down the stairs. "Can you answer the door please?"

Olivia hesitated, took a deep breath, and opened the front door.

Before her stood the Beasts, grinning like idiots. Olivia silently noted that their ill-fitting tuxes didn't make them look any less greasy.

"Hey, Vega," one said.

"What are you guys doing here?" said Olivia. "The ball doesn't start for another hour."

"We, uh, brought a guest," one of them replied. They pushed forward a boy Olivia hadn't noticed at first: Toby Decker.

Olivia knew him from math. He was wearing a gray suit with a blue polka-dot bow tie, and his blond hair was combed back from his forehead.

"Hi, Ivy. Thanks so much for having me," he said with formal politeness. Then he gestured to the Beasts. "These guys said you had more than enough punch, and it's going to be quite a party."

Olivia narrowed her eyes and turned to the Beast closest to her. "Can I speak to you for a moment?"

The boy shrugged, and Olivia led him down the hall. When they were just out of earshot, she spun around. "What are you doing?" she demanded.

"We brought our decoration—our human!" the boy said, bouncing up and down on his toes excitedly. "You know, like an hors d'oeuvre," he continued with a guffaw. "That means snack."

Olivia knew by now that there was only one way to handle Beastly behavior. She marched back to the front door, the boy scurrying after her, and went right up to Toby Decker.

"I'm sorry, Toby, but I'm afraid these boys misled you. Nobody can come tonight without an invitation. We're already over capacity."

"But—" Toby and a few of the Beasts began.

"No buts," Olivia said decisively. She glared over

Toby's shoulder at the Beasts. "It's a *safety* issue."

Then she turned back to Toby. "Sorry," she said as nicely as she could. "These guys should have known better. Maybe next time, okay?"

Toby nodded like he understood. Then he raised his eyebrows and said hopefully, "I should tell you I'm a really good dancer. I took classes for my older sister's sweet sixteen." He looked at Olivia expectantly.

"That's nice," said Olivia. "The boys will escort you back home now." And then she added, speaking very slowly and looking each of the Beasts right in the eye, "*And I'll see you at school on Monday, Toby.*"

Nobody moved. Olivia bore down on the Beasts with Ivy's death squint.

"Let's go," one of them sulked at last. They all turned and shuffled off down the hill, Toby trailing behind.

Olivia shut the door and smiled to herself. Like Ivy said, they weren't as scary as they smelled!

★ 🦇 ★

Ivy anxiously studied her reflection in the mirror that hung on an open door of her wardrobe. She straightened her dark, wine-colored, velvet strapless dress and turned around to inspect the thin satin ribbons crisscrossing her bare back. Her dark hair fell around her face in ringlets, and pearl earrings hung from her earlobes.

She was just applying her Midnight Merlot lipstick when she heard someone coming down the stairs.

"Hello?" she heard her sister whisper. "Ivy?"

Ivy pushed the wardrobe closed. Olivia stared.

"Do I look okay?" Ivy asked in a worried voice.

"You—you look . . ." Olivia stammered, "*unbelievable*!" She walked over, still staring.

"Really?" Ivy asked, glancing nervously in the mirror again.

"Really!" Olivia cried, circling her. "Brendan is going to be floored!"

"I hope so," Ivy said.

"I know so," Olivia said firmly.

Ivy couldn't help smiling. She pulled on a pair of long black evening gloves and looked at herself one last time in the mirror. *I look drop-dead*, she decided.

"I'd better put my own clothes back on and

scoot. You've got a ball to go to," Olivia said, grinning.

"Not so fast," said Ivy, barefooting it over to her bed, which was piled high with clothes, papers, and pillows. She rummaged through the mess, throwing clothes aside, until she emerged with a black box tied with a pink ribbon that she handed proudly to her sister.

"What's this?" Olivia asked, shaking the box.

"A thank-you gift," Ivy answered.

Olivia untied the ribbon. "For what?" she asked.

"For the last three weeks," Ivy told her. "For Brendan. For tonight. For being my sister." She shrugged. "For *everything*. Just open it."

Ivy watched Olivia's face as she reached into the box and took out a black baby tee. On it, the word "bunny" was printed in bubbly fuchsia letters, followed by a tiny sparkly bunny. Olivia gasped in delight. "I *love* it!" she exclaimed.

The doorbell rang. Ivy's heart leaped as she glanced at the clock by her bed. She guessed it must be Brendan, arriving early for pictures.

Olivia read her mind. "Where are your shoes?" she asked.

"Shoes?" Ivy grinned. "As if !" She hurried to lace up her best pair of high-heeled boots.

* 🐰 *

Olivia was tucked behind the suit of armor in the hall. Before she went home, she wanted to see Brendan's face when he arrived and saw Ivy in her ball dress. Ivy had said it was okay for her to watch for a few minutes, as long as she stayed out of sight. If Olivia looked through the gap between the breastplate and the arm piece, she could just see the front door.

She watched as Ivy opened the door and Brendan entered. He was wearing a black floor-length cape over his tuxedo and a textured white shirt with a white bow tie. His black curls shone.

"Ivy, you look beautiful!" Olivia heard Brendan say.

"Thank you," Ivy answered demurely.

From under his cape, he produced a flower: a single red rose, so dark it was almost black. Ivy took it and smiled as she looked at Brendan.

They looked at each other dreamily, and the moment was so romantic that Olivia thought they might kiss, but just then, Mr. Vega appeared.

"You must be Brendan," he said, descending the grand staircase. He looked impeccable in a black velvet tuxedo.

The doorbell rang again, and in rushed Sophia, wearing a beautiful black-and-white dress that looked like something from an Audrey Hepburn movie. She was also lugging a huge camera bag and a tripod. "Sorry I'm late." She panted. She stopped in her tracks and looked Brendan and Ivy up and down. "Wow, you two look killer!"

Olivia watched as Sophia took pictures of the perfect couple. In every single shot, Ivy did the one thing that Olivia liked to think she'd been responsible for teaching her to do. She smiled—and not a close-lipped Goth smile but a bright cheerleader beam!

When Ivy and Brendan, Mr. Vega and Sophia had left the hallway, Olivia slipped away down the staircase, back to Ivy's basement window. She needed to go home and get some rest. After all, cheerleading tryouts were in less than twenty-four hours, and Olivia needed to be ready for any-thing—especially if she was going to go head to head with Charlotte Brown.

CHAPTER 13

Ivy and Brendan sat with the rest of the planning committee at the table in the center of the ballroom. Melissa raised a glass of cherry punch and shouted over the din, "To Ivy, who seriously surprised us!"

"You're not kidding!" cried Sophia, flashing Ivy a knowing smile from where she stood. She lifted her camera and snapped a picture.

Ivy almost felt herself blush as she shyly clinked her glass against everyone else's. "I had a lot of help," she said.

"Miss Vega," a voice boomed. It was old Mr. Coleman, one of the chaperones, extending his hand. "This is the best All Hallows' Ball I have ever attended, and I have been at all two hundred two of them." He planted a cool kiss on the back of Ivy's hand. "You look smashing," he said.

Ivy let her eyes wander around the ballroom. Olivia really had done a killer job. People were marveling at the old film posters on the walls, and some were going from table to table having their friends take pictures of them with different celebrity tombstones. Everybody looked suave and mysterious, just like in the old vampire movies.

Suddenly, the room grew quieter. Ivy saw one of the Beasts standing in the center of the dance floor, a pale hand raised over his head to silence the crowd. In his other hand he held a black microphone.

Oh, no, thought Ivy. *What are they up to now?*

"Good eeeve-ning," the boy said, doing the lamest old-time vampire-accent imitation Ivy had ever heard. "I vant to invite you all onto zee dance floor for zee first dance."

Ivy couldn't help but laugh. The Beast was the DJ!

Brendan stood up. "Come on," he said, taking Ivy's hand. "It's the first dance."

Ivy shook her head. "We don't dance, remember?"

Brendan's eyes sparkled, and he leaned closer to her. "That's why they call it the *first* dance, Ivy," he said.

As Brendan led her onto the dance floor, his cape flowing around him, Ivy felt everyone's eyes on her. She saw people looking her up and down admiringly, and, at the edge of the dance floor, she even spotted her dad, beaming.

Brendan stopped right in the middle of the dance floor. Ivy put her head on his shoulder, and the song began. She closed her eyes. *I better not be dreaming*, she thought breathlessly.

* 🦇 *

Ivy woke up the next morning and pushed open her coffin. She hadn't dreamed any of it. She and Brendan had danced all through the ball. And afterward, they'd stayed up until one o'clock in the morning talking on the front porch.

She couldn't wait to call Olivia and tell her

all about it. After all, none of this would have happened without her. *Wait a minute,* Ivy thought, glancing at the clock. *Olivia's got cheerleading tryouts this morning!*

Ivy suddenly had a killer idea. She leaped out of bed and threw open one of her wardrobe doors. She would surprise her sister by supporting her from the bleachers during tryouts!

A half hour later, Ivy was marching through the front hall of Franklin Grove Middle School wearing the pinkest, most supportive outfit she could muster: a gray Devils sweatshirt and a Devils baseball cap pulled down over her hair.

She floated past her own reflection in the front hall display case. She almost looked like a cheerleader, with her school spirit costume.

As if on cue, a high-pitched voice called, "Olivia!"

Ivy looked up to see Charlotte Brown charging down the hallway, decked out in her cheerleading uniform.

"I've been looking for you everywhere, Olivia!" Charlotte complained.

Ivy almost corrected her, but then she thought

better of it and pulled her cap farther down over her eyes.

"Ms. Barnett told me to tell you that tryouts have been moved to the football field," Charlotte yelled. "The chess team is using the gym or something!"

"Really?" said Ivy perkily.

"You'd better get out there!" Charlotte said haughtily. "Ms. Barnett won't like it if you're late!" and, with that, she hurried away down the hall.

Oh, my goodness. I have to find Olivia right away, thought Ivy, *or she'll miss tryouts!*

She whipped out her phone and dialed Olivia's cell, but there was no answer. She glanced at the clock on the wall: 11:21. That meant Ivy had only nine minutes to find her sister.

Ivy ran to check the girls' locker room. The only people she found inside were Katie and Allison, decked out in full-on cheer gear.

"Hi, Olivia!" they said in unison.

Ivy spun around without answering. She ran back to the other side of school, and checked Olivia's locker—nothing. She ran on to the science hall bathroom—also nothing. The situation was starting to seem grave. Ivy tried Olivia's cell phone again. When that didn't work, she tried her sister at home.

"Hello?" said Olivia's dad.

"Hi, Mr. Abbott, it's Ivy, Olivia's friend from school," Ivy explained.

"Well, good morning, Ivy. What can I do for you?"

"Is Olivia there?" Ivy panted.

"'Fraid not," he answered. "The cheerleading tryouts are right about now."

"Right," Ivy said sheepishly. "Thanks." She ended the call and slumped against the bathroom counter.

Her sister was nowhere to be found. Ivy glanced at the screen on her cell phone: 11:25. Only five minutes left to go.

This can't be happening, Ivy thought with a shake of her head. *Not after all Olivia and I have done.*

She pulled off her hat, and spun around to face the mirror. In her locker there was a can of spray-on tan, which Olivia had accidentally left in Ivy's bag after their first switch. Ivy thought she could put her hair in a ponytail and make it to the field before it was too late.

But what if somebody notices that there are two Olivia's running around school? Ivy wondered.

It's a risk I have to take, she decided.

She ran to her locker, grabbed the spray-on tan, and dashed back to the bathroom. Then she quickly applied the spray, and was tying her hair into a ponytail when she realized that she didn't have pom-poms. *Ms. Barnett will freak!* Ivy thought.

She threw open the door to one of the stalls and saw two rolls of toilet paper sitting on the back of the toilet. *They're not the best poms in the world,* thought Ivy, *and I probably won't get away with this, but it's the best I can do.*

A roll of toilet paper in either hand, Ivy charged onto the sports field, but the only people there were two jocks tossing a football back and forth. There were no cheerleaders in sight.

Ivy looked around, confused. "Excuse me," she said. "Do you know if cheerleading tryouts are supposed to be here right now?"

"In the gym," one of the boys grunted, looking bemusedly at Ivy and her toilet roll poms.

And all at once, Ivy understood what had happened. Charlotte had lied, hoping that Olivia would show up in the wrong place and miss tryouts. *The fiend*! Ivy thought.

She hastily tossed a roll of toilet paper to each of the boys and ran back toward the gym, thinking what a stroke of luck it had been that she hadn't reached Olivia on her cell. As she ran, she chanted to herself through clenched teeth. "When you're up, you're up . . . when you're down, you're down . . . when you're messing with my sister . . . you're upside down!"

Ivy stood outside the gym door and peeked in through the window. Sure enough, there was Olivia, cheering her heart out at the center of the formation. Charlotte Brown cheered beside her, the peeved look in her eyes belying the fake smile on her face.

$\star$ 🐰 $\star$

Olivia pushed through the door of the Meat & Greet Diner and rushed to the back of the restaurant, where she spotted everyone waiting for her

196

in Ivy's booth. Sitting across from Camilla and Sophia, Brendan had his arm draped around Ivy's shoulder.

Olivia couldn't contain herself a moment longer. "I made the squad!" she shouted before she'd even reached their table. Everyone in the diner spun around to look.

Oops, thought Olivia. Her friends burst out laughing.

"I made the squad!" she said again in an exaggerated whisper.

"Congratulations!" Ivy cheered. Camilla and Sophia clapped.

"Ivy said you were deadly at tryouts," Brendan told her.

Sophia held up crossed fingers. "Can we call you captain?"

"Not this year," Olivia admitted. "Charlotte's captain. But that's only fair, since she's been on the squad the longest."

"And she's so great at telling people what to do," Ivy added.

"Exactly." Olivia grinned. "Anyway, it just means I'll be able to spend more time with my friends!" Olivia looked around the table at Camilla, Sophia, Ivy, and Brendan. She felt really happy.

The waitress appeared. "Tofu burger with salad?" she asked.

"You bet," Olivia replied, smiling. Then she announced to the table, "I'll be right back. I'm going to go change." After all, she was still wearing her cheerleader uniform, and she was dying to get Ivy alone. She winked at her sister meaningfully.

The moment Ivy followed her through the bathroom door, Olivia said, "How did it go last night!?"

They debriefed as Olivia took off her cheerleader outfit and put on her new favorite baby tee. When Ivy told her about the first dance with Brendan, it nearly took Olivia's breath away.

"This is the best weekend of my life," Ivy finished.

"I feel the same way!" Olivia agreed.

"I think our biological parents would be seriously proud of us," Ivy said.

I just wish we knew them, Olivia thought with a pang.

"Let's make a pact," Ivy suggested.

"A vampire pact?" asked Olivia.

"No." Ivy rolled her eyes. "A pact between us. A sisterhood pact."

Olivia understood. Cheerleading, dating, the ball—it had all been fun, but there was something more important.

Ivy took her necklace off and pressed her emerald ring against the one on Olivia's finger. "We pledge to be there for each other," she said.

"Day or night," Olivia put in solemnly.

"In darkness and light," Ivy went on. "We pledge to stick—"

"Together," Olivia finished for her. And then she reached out to hug her twin sister. And as Ivy hugged her back, she knew that they both had tears in their eyes.

Don't miss Ivy and Olivia's next adventure in My Sister the Vampire #2: Fangtastic!

Ivy Vega trudged sleepily into the breakfast room, slid into her chair, and rested her cheek on the cool stone table. She wished she was still in her coffin. Monday mornings were the worst.

"Good morning, sleepybones," her father said, placing a bowl next to her head.

"Shh," Ivy murmured, her eyes closed. "I'm still sleeping."

"It's your favorite," her dad coaxed. "Marshmallow Platelets."

Ivy peered at the little white marshmallows and maroon bits bobbing in their milky sea. "Thanks," she mumbled.

Her father, already dressed for work in black chinos and a black pin-striped shirt with French cuffs, sipped his tea and picked up the remote control. "There is nothing better for a young person's dull morning mind," he said, "than dull morning television."

He flipped through the weather and some talk shows before settling on *The Morning Star*.

"Please no," Ivy said. "Just looking at Serena Star's smile gives me sunburn."

Serena Star, WowTV's best celebrity reporter, had impossibly bright, bleached blond hair and eyes that looked as if they'd been surgically enhanced to be permanently wide open in either adoration or shock. Lately she'd been trying to cast herself as a serious journalist on her own morning news show, *The Morning Star*. Just the other day, Ivy had turned the TV off in exasperation after Serena had said, "Tell me, Mr. Senator, how does it feel to have a law named after you?"

This morning, Serena Star was standing with her back to a small crowd of people, talking into her microphone. She was wearing a tiny blue suede miniskirt under a knee-length trench coat, and the look in her wide eyes said "shock!" She was in a park or maybe a graveyard. A scruffy, black-clad teenager stood beside her—

Ivy's dad flipped the channel.

"Turn back!" Ivy blurted.

"But you said—"

"I know. Turn back!" she repeated.

Ivy could not believe her eyes. The boy standing next to Serena Star was none other than Garrick Stephens, one of the lamest vampires at her school. He and his bonehead friends—everyone called them the Beasts—were always pulling dumb stunts, like seeing which one of them could eat the most garlic croutons without getting seriously ill. They weren't nearly as scary as they smelled, but they'd been annoying since forever.

Serena Star looked squarely at the camera. "I, Serena Star, now bring you an exclusive interview with the thirteen-year-old boy who was almost buried alive. I think you'll agree it's a story that's truly . . . INDEADIBLE!" A graphic with the word "INDEADIBLE!" materialized on the screen over Garrick's head, and Ivy rolled her eyes. Serena was always making up lame words for her on-screen headlines.

"Awesome!" Garrick Stephens grinned.

Ivy's head ached. *How in the underworld,* she thought, *are we going to cover up a vampire popping out of a coffin in the middle of a funeral?*